In the Florida Keys, life is full of perfect sunsets, warm evening breezes and hot days in the surf.... Days that only get hotter when romance is in the air....

Indulge in...

Body Heat Lori Foster
He thought she was shy? *Ha!* Melanie turned to Adam with a scathing retort when she remembered his state of undress. *Oh, my!* Her lips wouldn't move. Nor would her eyes. They were glued on his hard body. Her imagination hadn't done him justice....

Slow Burn Elda Minger
Ally loved the way Flynn was looking at her. With intent and purpose. She'd never been alone with a purely male animal like him. She owed Flynn nothing. *Yet she had the feeling she was in for the best sex she'd ever had in her life....*

Dear Reader,

We have a special treat for you this month! Two deliciously sexy BLAZE stories in *one* volume. Popular authors Lori Foster and Elda Minger team up to deliver two sizzling tales about heroes and heroines who decide to indulge in summer flings—with heated results!

Both Lori and Elda enjoy writing for Temptation BLAZE. They welcome the creativity and challenge of telling a more sensuous story. And it's clear our readers love what they and our other BLAZE authors do. BLAZE has been, well, a *blazing* success. We look forward to bringing you more books each and every month.

Meantime, kick back, grab an ice-cold drink and get ready to dive into *Sizzle!* You'll be glad you did!

Happy Reading,

Birgit Davis-Todd
Senior Editor

P.S. We love to hear from our readers. Write to us at:
Harlequin Enterprises Limited
225 Duncan Mill Road
Don Mills, Ontario
Canada
M3B 3K9

SIZZLE!
Lori Foster &
Elda Minger

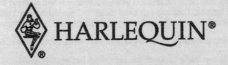

HARLEQUIN®

TORONTO • NEW YORK • LONDON
AMSTERDAM • PARIS • SYDNEY • HAMBURG
STOCKHOLM • ATHENS • TOKYO • MILAN • MADRID
PRAGUE • WARSAW • BUDAPEST • AUCKLAND

ISBN 0-373-25839-9

SIZZLE!

Copyright © 1999 Harlequin Books S.A.
BODY HEAT
Copyright © 1999 by Lori Foster.
SLOW BURN
Copyright © 1999 by Elda Minger.

This edition published by arrangement with Harlequin Books S.A.

® and TM are trademarks of the publisher. Trademarks indicated with ® are registered in the United States Patent and Trademark Office, the Canadian Trade Marks Office and in other countries.

Visit us at www.romance.net

Printed in U.S.A.

BODY HEAT
Lori Foster

Lori Foster had a lot of fun writing *Body Heat*. Researching Florida helped her make new friends on the Internet, and now she's determined to take a vacation there soon. With her family, of course. She married her high school sweetheart, the funniest, most supportive man she knows. He and their three wonderful sons keep her happily on the brink of insanity. Luckily Lori likes being a little zany—and a little risqué, as her books prove.

Lori's five bestselling Temptation BLAZE titles have left readers wanting more, and they won't be disappointed. This is one busy lady!

In September 1999 look for Lori's new novel, *Beguiled,* paired with *The Private Eye* by Jayne Ann Krentz—a special treat marking Harlequin's 50th Anniversary. Then in October Lori is back at Temptation with a spin-off to *Beguiled* called *Wanton* (#752) and more...

Fans will also be thrilled with the prospect of a four-book Temptation miniseries by Lori coming up in the year 2000, and her exciting debut with Harlequin Duets!

SHE WAS THE ONLY female fully clothed.

On an enormous party boat filled with people, a dozen half-naked women vying for masculine attention, her subtlety made her stand out. And he wasn't the only man noticing, a fact that was starting to get to him.

He should thank her. After all, he needed all the distractions he could get right now. Trying to keep his mind off the importance of the deal he'd finalize once they reached Marco Island was making him crazy. He'd worked long and hard for this day, and now it was almost at hand.

She walked to the railing, leaning out over the clear blue Gulf waters, watching the sky and the endless seas; she seemed aloof. A damp, salty breeze picked up and plastered her loose, colorful skirts to her body, emphasizing a sweet little bottom and long legs.

Adam Stone shifted his carry-on bag from one hand to the other, then flexed his fingers. The expensive leather bag, bought for him by his younger brother, Kyle, was a celebratory gift specifically for this trip. The bag was attached to his belt by a long leather strap, securing it to his person. It held important papers as well as a sizable check. Beyond that, the bag held significant sentimental value. This bag was a sign of his future, his family's future. There was little chance of being robbed on the yacht, but his innate sense of caution was hard to shake off when so much was at stake.

He considered approaching the woman, but held back, mostly because he knew he didn't have time to get involved beyond small talk. Not only that, she appeared to be ignoring all the males on the boat, himself included. So far, she'd kept her back to him, almost as if she knew of his interest and rejected it out of hand.

The Florida sun was hazy today, the sky overcast, but that didn't deter the bikini-clad boaters who approached him. They'd been coming on to him since he'd climbed aboard, determinedly seductive, despite his disinterest. All his attention remained centered on that elusive woman as she walked away, separating herself from the crowd once again.

Without his usual charm, Adam excused himself to follow her. It was her glossy black hair he spotted first. Even without the glare of sunshine, that dark hair shone silky soft. The wind ruffled the short, fine curls and sent her colorful skirts billowing like a flag.

Adam swallowed.

Ridiculous that seeing the shape of a slim thigh through a filmy skirt should have such an effect when he'd just walked away from a topless woman, but there was no denying his interest. He felt it clear to the bottom of his stomach, and somehow, the feeling was damn familiar.

Her elbows were braced on the handrail, so he could easily trace the feminine line of her nape, her spine, down to a narrow waist. Her halter top, modest in comparison to the tiny bikinis, still afforded him a teasing view of honey-colored skin and tempting curves. Enthralled, he stepped a little closer, again shifting the bag in his hand.

She hadn't yet noticed his approach. With a sigh that he detected even over the loud music and the rush of the water against the hull, she lifted her face to the breeze. Adam stepped slightly to the side, curious to see her profile, to decide if her looks warranted all the interest she'd generated in him.

His shock almost knocked him over.

"Mel? Mel Tucker?"

Rather than turning to him with equal surprise, she abruptly stiffened. Her hands gripped the rail a little harder, and she slowly swiveled her head in his direction. Eyes narrow, mouth set, she said, "Old habits die hard, I see. But the name is Melanie. Ms. Tucker to you."

Adam laughed, his entire mood suddenly lighter. The cursed fate that had put him on this boat no longer seemed so cursed. "You haven't changed a bit, Mel." His gaze coasted over her as she turned to face him fully, hands on her slim hips. His voice dropped the tiniest bit, and without his mind's permission, he muttered, "You're still sexy as hell."

Her mouth tightened, and the pale blue eyes that still haunted his dreams looked more ominous than the approaching storm. Lifting her nose slightly in a gesture she'd perfected as far back as grade school, she said, "You obviously haven't changed, either."

Her words hit him like a blow—just as she'd no doubt intended. His muscles knotted. The *hell* he hadn't changed. He had—in too many ways to count.

Adam held onto the burst of anger by a thread. Always, for as long as he could remember, Mel had been able to rile him with very little effort. The last time he'd seen her back in Brockton, Ohio, his family had been incredibly poor, while *her* family owned the entire town. She lived on a hill with a view while he lived down by the river in a trailer nearly rusted through. Though he'd gotten a job at a young age, what he made went into helping out his folks—and his father had died anyway. Mel had gone off to an elite college, and he'd dealt with some of the worst grief of his life.

And she dared to suggest he'd survived it all without changing?

Because he was older and wiser and had long since outgrown taunting any lady, he forced a smile. "Seven years have gone by. I think it's safe to say we've both changed."

She blinked hard and her jaw worked. "What do you want, Adam?"

Incredulous, he stared at her, his mouth open, his brows up. "You're still angry," he accused. "After seven years, you're holding a grudge!" He finished with a short, rough laugh that sent her back straight and her chin up.

Several tense seconds passed, then she abruptly turned away and marched the last few feet to the very back of the boat. She ducked under a slide that sloped from the upper deck to just above the water, opened a double gate and sat on the dive platform. Gathering up her skirts to her knees, she plunked her small feet into the blue water, dismissing him.

Adam fumed. The hell she would dismiss him! He, too, ducked under the slide, sitting cross-legged beside her and propping his bag in his lap. She remained silent and stiff. Too silent. He didn't like it.

Mel had always had an undeniable effect on him. From the first time he'd seen her, when they'd both been no more than kids, there'd been a chemistry of sorts, something she'd denied and he'd continually struggled with. He felt it still, but he wouldn't let her know. He wouldn't let her and her wealth and social position intimidate him after all this time. He'd done all right for himself, though it hadn't been easy. He had no reason to feel like the poor trash her family had once looked down on.

The boat moved lazily, barely slicing through the Gulf waters, yet the surface was choppy. He glanced at the sky, then frowned at Melanie. Searching for innocuous conversation to show his nonchalance, he murmured, "It looks like a damn storm. I'm going to be late."

He wanted her to ask him, Late for what? But she didn't, of course. Nothing with Mel had ever been easy. Instead she said, "You shouldn't be on this boat, Adam."

She hadn't looked at him, and that bothered him even more. All his life he'd thought of her as the one that got away, the one out of reach. There were still nights when he couldn't sleep for thinking of her, imagining....

When they were younger, he'd teased her unmercifully. Though he was two years older, he'd been held back in first grade after missing too much school due to illnesses that didn't get treated by a doctor. Real doctors were often too expensive, and trips to the clinic took his parents away from work.

He and Mel saw each other often back then, and her life-style, her obvious wealth, had been like a pounding toothache; it prodded at him always, reminding him of what he didn't have, while she had way too much. As a kid, he'd almost hated her, at least on some level.

By junior high school, though, he'd learned to hide

his feelings...and he'd gradually become aware of her as a female. She represented all the things in life he wanted to obtain; security, comfort, importance. After a while, he'd wanted to obtain *her*. But that was like wanting the moon in the palm of his hand. Ridiculous.

He'd watched her constantly, dwelling on their differences, feeling equal parts obsessive and possessive. When her innocent eyes began looking more sad, more lonely, he was the first, maybe the only, to notice. In a small, moderate town, her outstanding wealth had isolated her.

He'd wanted to chase that sadness away. It gave them something in common, something he gravitated to.

But that was so long ago. She'd hated him then.

Evidently she hated him still.

"I should have taken a charter," he growled, ignoring the pang of old regrets and the bite of her scorn that could still bother him regardless of his denials. The wind whistled around them, and a colorful float went flying off the deck to bob wildly in the churning water. "But the damn captain of the charter came down ill. I would have missed an important meeting, but then your buddy, the captain of this boat, saw me and offered a ride. I accepted."

"He's not my buddy. I barely know him."

"Then what are you doing here?"

She stared out at sea, constantly pushing her wind-tossed curls out of her face. Her hair was shorter now, but he liked it. The casual style suited her small features. The hem of her skirt was getting damp, but she either didn't notice or didn't care. He noticed. He'd always been painfully aware of every little detail that concerned her.

Ignoring his question, she said, "I saw you earlier." She glanced at him, then away again, her expression still set. "You've had at least two women hanging onto you ever since you stepped on board. Some things, I guess, never change."

Stunned, he stared at her profile. "You saw me right away but didn't say hello?"

"Why would I?" She looked right at him, and her eyes blazed. "We didn't exactly part as friends. You were a mean, petty jerk who enjoyed making my life miserable."

He searched her face, his frustration extreme. "For God's sake, Mel, that was seven years ago. We were kids, and when we got older I didn't..."

"Melanie. My name is Melanie, damn it."

He couldn't recall ever seeing her temper before. Mostly she'd been nervous with him, shying away if he got too close, never defending herself, no matter how hard he'd tried to get her to do just that. He lifted one brow, more frustrated by the second. "Well, excuse me all to hell and back." Then he asked, "You have changed, haven't you?"

There went that chin again. "If you mean you no longer intimidate me, yes."

"I intimidated you?" He knew it was true, that he'd played on her vulnerability, but it wasn't something he wanted to own up to now. Jealousy, need, a very basic emotional hunger, had driven him then. He wasn't proud of that time in his life. "Honey, you were the one with all the clout. If you'd wanted, you could have had my whole family tossed out of town."

She blinked, as if surprised by what she'd said, what she'd admitted. A few raindrops fell, lightly at first, but quickly picking up ferocity. Behind them, the partyers began scurrying about, laughing and squealing. Women grabbed for their tops or towels, couples jumped out of the upper deck hot tub. Within minutes, everyone was under cover in the cabin. Everyone except them.

Finally Melanie looked away and Adam drew a deep, starving breath, still watching her. For a minute there, with her gaze locked on his, he'd felt caught, and the feeling wasn't altogether uncomfortable. She stirred something in him that had been missing for quite some time.

The rain came a little harder, wetting his hair, but Adam ignored it.

He should take her arm and help her into the cabin. But he didn't want to. He wanted to talk to her, alone, away from the damn drunken crowd. Once they reached the island, he likely wouldn't see her again. Somehow, he wanted to apologize to her for his behavior of the past. Somehow, he wanted her to know all he'd accomplished since then, exactly how much he'd changed.

He didn't want her thinking of him as the poor kid down by the river.

The boat was suddenly put in full throttle, and they both lurched, grabbing a section of handrail—and a part of each other. Mel's fingers clutched his pant leg while he held her elbow. Gently, his heart pounding, he slid his hand down her arm to her slender fingers. Her hold loosened, and when she would have let go, he captured her hand, steadying her. Mel's eyes widened and she looked behind her, as if only then aware of the storm and the deserted deck. The bouncing boat kept her from shaking him off. Over the roar of the engine, she said, "We should go inside."

An abandoned beach towel hit him in the back, plastered to him by the rain and wind. He held her just a little tighter while struggling to untangle himself from it. Thank God he had dry clothes in his bag or his meeting would be ruined. He couldn't exactly make the deal of his life looking like a drowned rat. Another float whipped by, disappearing into the churning waters.

Growing alarmed by the strength of the wind, Adam carefully stood, then helped her to do the same. From the sound of the revelers inside the cabin, the laughing and loud music, no one even knew they were still on deck. And just as Mel got to her feet, the boat veered sharply to port and she lost her balance. With wide eyes and a horrified scream, she crashed overboard. Adam cursed viciously and made a wild grab for her but missed. His bag fell from his grasp, and the strap to his waist jerked him off balance. He, too, went over with a gigantic splash, but more awkwardly than she, his head hitting the slide as he flew past.

Just before he went under, he heard the roar of the receding boat motor, the louder roar of the storm, and worse, Mel's nearly hysterical screams. Her fear galvanized him. Ignoring his aching head, he pushed himself to the surface and frantically searched for her while wind, rain and waves lashed his face. The side of his head hurt like hell, but he didn't have time to complain yet. Mel was already several yards away from him, thrashing about wildly as if drowning. Adam felt a crushing fear when he twisted to see the boat going out of sight. Fighting the dragging weight of his heavy bag, he began stroking through the water toward her. Just as she let out another garbled scream, he reached her...and they both went under.

MELANIE FELT A SLICK, sliding movement against her lower body and opened her mouth to scream again. She managed to gulp a mouthful of salt water. Visions of sharks made her panic real and unmanageable.

But then Adam's blond head broke the surface, and he dragged her upward against his solid body. "Mel!" She felt his legs brush her, tangling with her long skirts, his hard arms around her. Nothing in her life had ever felt so reassuring.

"Oh, God." She gripped him fiercely, trying her best to ignore the reality of her situation. She loved boats, the sunshine and fresh air, but she had never quite envisioned herself thrown overboard, at the mercy of the Gulf and all its aquatic denizens. "Oh, God, oh, God…"

"Mel, you're drowning me! It's okay."

He tried to ease her away, but she got one hand knotted in his hair and held on for dear life. His familiar scent, one she'd never forget no matter how long she lived, surrounded her, and she crowded even closer. His hair was the same, still too long, too sexy, damn him, and she used it like an anchor, holding him tight. She didn't want to be shark bait.

Her voice shook uncontrollably when she spoke. "Where's the damn boat? Where is it!?"

"Sh. It's all right," he said. "We need to swim, honey."

"Swim? *Swim!*" A vicious wave slapped her in the face, water going up her nose, making her choke and sputter. The furious storm continued, almost pushing them under. Would the turbulent water draw the sharks or chase them away?

Shouting to be heard, Adam said, "The boat is gone. Mel, loosen up, you're ripping my hair out."

She tried, she really did. She'd so badly wanted to make a good impression on him, and this surely wasn't it. But she couldn't get her fingers to unknot. "This isn't happening…this isn't happening…."

"Mel, calm down. The idiots on board are either too drunk or too stupid to realize they lost us. We're on our own until they dock and count heads."

If they counted heads. He was right about them all being tipsy, and she'd so deliberately separated herself from them, wanting to be alone, needing the solitude. Would they even notice she was gone? She moaned long and loud. "We'll drown!"

"No, we won't." His voice was calm, sure, just as she remembered it. "We're not far from shore. Can you swim?"

"What about sharks?" She looked around wildly, terrified, not certain if what she saw were shadows in the water or merely waves.

"There's no sharks here."

Her head whipped back around, and she tightened her hand in his hair, making him wince. "How do you know?" she demanded, shaking his head, wanting confirmation. It would be just like Adam to pull her leg, to play on her fear.

"Mel, damn it, turn me loose!"

Through her panic, she read the pain on his face and struggled to relax her grip. Adam circled her waist with his strong arms and held her closer. The contact with his body startled her, despite her predicament. Always, when she'd imagined such a scenario, they'd been on dry land, he'd been filled with abject apologies, and she'd been benevolent in her forgiveness.

Instead, she managed to make a total fool of herself. Not that it mattered if they were going to die, anyway.

Speaking close to her ear, he said, "I've got a Florida guidebook, *The Key to the Keys.* No sharks in these waters, I promise. Now can you swim?"

"Don't let me go!"

"Honey, I'm right here. But we need—"

Something bumped into them. It was huge and…red. She gasped, again choking.

"A float, surely heaven sent." Adam smiled at her, his eyes narrowed against the impact of the waves, his lashes spiked with the rain and sea, his blond hair plastered to his skull. But he smiled, and she felt ridiculously reassured as she treaded water. "Mel? Can you climb on?"

She remembered the float blowing off the deck, and he had offered it to her. Lord love him. She gratefully grabbed the rubber edge and with more panic than grace heaved her body mostly upon it. She gripped it so tightly, there was no way she'd lose her hold until she felt solid land beneath her feet. Her wet, clinging skirts were everywhere, and whether or not they covered her backside, she couldn't say. She felt too numb to know, too frightened to care.

She felt Adam rearrange the skirt, felt his hands on her flesh and merely said a prayer that they'd survive.

"Now just hang on." Moving to the back, Adam levered himself up over her until his head was even with her derriere. She felt his heavy, sodden leather case placed on the small of her back but didn't begrudge him that. As long as she was out, she was happy to accommodate him. He began paddling and kicking, propelling them forward.

She felt like an ineffectual idiot, like a hysterical dolt, but she couldn't seem to help herself. She continued to look around, watching for signs of creatures of any kind. If she spotted so much as a goldfish eye to eye, she'd lose her fragile grasp on control.

A thought occurred to her, and she yelled over the storm, "How do you know which way to go?"

"I'm guessing."

"What!" He mumbled something she couldn't hear and his chin bumped her bottom, then he shouted, "The guidebook, remember? I figure we're still somewhere between the Keys and Marco Island. Trust me, I know what I'm doing."

She thought to question him further but decided against it. Talking was too difficult at the moment, and her teeth were chattering too badly to make good sense anyway. It was easier to trust him and let him take over.

But when it seemed like an hour had gone by and her lips were numb from the cold rain, she began to panic again. He could well be swimming them farther out into the Gulf, rather than inland. There could be whales as well as sharks, maybe even giant eels— She jumped when he reached up and touched her cheek.

"Almost there, Mel. How're you holding up?"

For a moment she couldn't believe what he'd said, then, incredulous, she asked, "Almost *where?*"

"Shore. Look ahead."

He had better eyes than she if he could penetrate the sheet of rain, but when she looked as hard as she could, she thought she could see the outline of land. Her breath left her in a whoosh, and her heart began racing. "Where are we?"

"Damned if I know. But if it'll be solid beneath my feet, then it's good enough for me."

Absolutely. She wanted out of the water and she didn't care where. With a deep breath to fortify her, she released her death grip on the raft. Her knuckles hurt, her fingers felt stiff, but she extended her arms and began paddling.

"Good girl. We'll get there, Mel. You'll see."

She kept paddling, but she closed her eyes, too, saying a silent prayer. *Please, please, please let me live long enough to put my feet on land again.*

Almost ten minutes later, her prayers were answered.

2

WHEN SHE REALIZED Adam was standing, she almost cried with relief. She wanted to slide off the raft to make it easier for him, but the rain had let up and she could see more clearly. The land they approached looked ominous with an abundance of skinny, mangled palm trees, some practically hanging in the water, and spreading, spidery mangrove trees, making the island look more like a scraggly forest. The ocean floor was visible, and what she saw scared her to death. Shells, small fish, water weeds. She curled a little more tightly on the raft.

"Do you think there's...*anything* in the water?"

At first Adam didn't answer, just kept trudging forward, dragging her along. Finally, with weariness evident in every word, he said, "Nothing's bit me yet."

Just the thought made her squeamish. A few more feet, and Adam walked past her, going the rest of the way to shore and collapsing onto his back.

Alarmed, Mel realized the raft couldn't very well be dragged in with her on it, and if she didn't move, she'd float right back out to sea. Not that he seemed to care.

Mustering her courage, she jumped off the raft—and sank as deep as mid-shins. The water was so shallow, Adam couldn't have pulled her any farther along.

Disregarding her blatant cowardice even as she carefully surveyed the shallow water, she attempted to act blasé, to hide her fear. She grabbed the raft and pulled it behind her as she waded out of the water.

Her strappy little sandals were long gone, and her toes sank into the white sand. Her skirts, made to wrap twice around her waist, were sadly tangled, sticking wetly to her thighs, hindering her every movement. She stopped to shake them loose, to squeeze out some of the water, but it was useless. They clung to her like a second skin. She plopped down on the fine sand beside Adam. He didn't move.

His eyes were closed against the now gentle rain, his clothes every bit as ruined as hers, his mouth tight. And still he looked incredibly gorgeous.

All the old feelings of inadequacy swamped her. For as long as she could remember, Adam had been vital, outgoing, easily the center of attention whenever he entered a room. And she'd been a fading wallflower, crippled by her vulnerability and shyness. When she'd seen him on the boat, she'd begun reviving plans to show him how she'd changed, to prove she wasn't the little girl he probably remembered with pity. She'd thought to wait until they'd docked, change into something more sophisticated and then approach him.

Instead, he'd approached her, taking her totally off guard, and she'd behaved like an idiot. "Adam?"

"Hmm?" He looked a little pale, his mouth pinched.

"Are you all right?"

"Just dandy. I always take an hour-long swim to get the old blood pumping."

Her eyes narrowed. Just like him to be so sarcastic at a moment like this.

But then she realized he had to be worn out. To her shame, she hadn't helped him a bit. She looked at him again and considered apologizing, but couldn't decide how. He was still her high-school nemesis, yet now he was her hero, as well. The circumstances had her grinding her teeth.

She looked around, up and down the shoreline, and saw nothing but bent and twisted trees, sand, a few pelicans. The island wasn't large by any stretch, and she wondered how it would fare if the storm returned. "Adam..."

He groaned and reached up to rub at his head. "Talk softly, okay? I've got a ringing headache."

She lowered her voice appropriately. "Do you have any idea where we are?"

"Not a clue."

She looked around again. It was a safe bet they weren't on Marco Island, so it had to be one of the smaller islands. She started to stand, her intent to locate people, houses, anything that looked even remotely domestic or civilized. But Adam caught at her arm.

"No, don't wander off. I don't want to take the chance we'll get separated. Just give me a few minutes and we'll start exploring together." He said it all with his eyes closed, and her concern for him doubled despite her resentment of the situation.

Sinking into the sand, she looked him over. He lay on the shore like a starfish, arms and legs spread, his posture one of complete exhaustion. His tie remained tight around his throat, his bag still attached to his belt. Melanie figured the least she could do was try to make him comfortable, to prove he no longer cowed her. And he had jumped in after her, had kept her safe. If it hadn't been for him, the sharks—she gulped—probably would have had her for lunch. Though she hadn't actually seen any sharks, she was still certain they were there. And if nothing else, his presence had given her immeasurable comfort.

She reached for the strap on his bag, but before she could get a good grip on it, his fingers bit into her wrist.

His eyes opened and they pinned her, hot and intense. "What do you think you're doing?"

Uh-oh. Melanie remembered those eyes from high school, so compelling, so sexy. Adam Stone had always had the ability to turn females into mush. Though he'd been poor and oftentimes dangerous, women had gravitated to him in hordes. But she'd resisted. She'd had little choice. His only interest in her had been spite.

"I was going to move your bag and undo your tie."

"Why?" The visible signs of exhaustion momentarily left his body, and he looked ready to attack.

She made a sound of disgust. "You look miserable, that's why."

"Like you care?" He snorted. "Aren't you the same woman who just a while ago was ready to bite off my face?"

She blushed, annoyed that he'd point that out. Damn him, how did he constantly do this to her? They'd only been reunited a very short time, and already she was on the defensive! Since she'd first met him, it had been that way. Right before she'd left for college, he tried to pretend an interest in her, but she'd been wise to him by then. She knew he was only setting her up so he could humiliate her. She'd refused him as quietly and with as little confrontation as possible.

But she'd come home from college a changed woman. Away from her parents' smothering influence, she'd grown into her own, able to stand up to anyone when the situation warranted. She'd anxiously looked forward to her next meeting with Adam Stone, anxiously practiced all the things she'd say to him, how she'd put him in his place.

How she'd make him see her as more than a pawn.

Only he was gone by then, moved away after his father's death. And she'd forever felt cheated of her big moment.

She'd never forgotten him; she doubted she ever would. Other than her parents, he'd had more influence in her life than any other person.

Damn him, she would not let him do this to her again! She was a mature businesswoman, and she'd behave as such, no matter his provocation.

With her hands fisted in her ruined skirts, she forced a calm tone and said, "I was trying to be cordial, Adam, considering you played the gallant and rescued me."

He scowled. "What the hell are you talking about?"

"You dove in after me," she reminded him. "You didn't have to do that, all things considered. The least I can do now is try to be nice."

He stared, his expression stunned. "Nice?" Then he laughed and dropped his head onto the sand with a groan. He was silent a moment before muttering, "Well, what do you know. You owe me."

"I didn't say that."

"Didn't you? It's appropriate, don't you think? My clothes are ruined, and it's for certain I've missed my damned meeting." He cocked an eye open to look at her. "All because I jumped in to save you."

"Don't curse."

Coming up on one elbow, he growled, "I'll damn well curse if I want to! You have no idea what missing that meeting means."

She leaned back, away from the force of his anger. Subdued just a bit, she said, "So tell me."

He glared at her, then turned his head away. After a second, he plopped back on the sand. "Forget it."

She shrugged, but since he wasn't watching her, he didn't see it. Guilt gnawed at her. "I suppose I do owe you. A little."

"A *lot*."

She sighed. "Very well. I owe you a lot. How much money will you be out because of our...misfortune?"

His gaze turned lethal, and the words were little more than a whisper. "You're not going to offer me money, are you sweetheart?"

"But you said I owed you."

"You owe me gratitude, that's all. I don't want your damn money."

"Oh." The money would have been so much easier.

He shifted, putting one arm behind his head, watching her, a half smile on his sensuous mouth. "Okay, Mel, since we're agreed, have at it."

"Excuse me?"

"Go ahead and make me comfortable. That was your original intent, right? I await your efforts."

He said it like a dare, and her temper pricked. She would not let him, or any other man, intimidate her ever again. So what that he was more muscled now, that maturity made him even more masculine, more sexy? His blond hair was streaked from hours in the sun; his eyes were dark gold. He looked incredible, while she knew she looked a wreck.

It was bad enough that he'd spotted her in the casual outfit she'd chosen for the boat. Her halter and loose, lingerie-style shorts were made of the same silky material, and covered by the long, thin skirts, but she'd still felt too physically exposed to face him. The cabin had been too crowded to hide in, and then she'd realized she didn't want to hide from him. Not ever again. But she thought he'd be too involved with the women swarming him to notice her.

She'd obviously been wrong.

Now, after her ordeal, she looked wretched. She could feel her eye makeup smeared on her cheeks, knew her short hair stuck out at all angles. She'd lost even more weight over the years; while he was thick with muscle, she was lacking the lush curves men seemed to admire, and in her outfit, there was no way to disguise her figure.

But she couldn't change any of that, so she'd simply have to make the best of an awkward, unimaginable situation.

Mustering her courage, she again reached for his bag. Unfortunately, it couldn't be unlatched at the handle; it had to be undone at his belt. The front of his belt. Without looking, she could sense Adam's smirk. He didn't think she'd do it; she intended to prove him wrong.

To distract herself from his body, she said, "It's finally stopped raining." She slid her fingers under his belt and tried to work the latch.

"It's going to get hot as hell, you know."

She felt the heat already. Adam's stomach was solid rock against the backs of her fingers. And warm. Very warm in comparison to his clammy clothes.

"Humid, too," he added more softly, his voice a rough growl. "Downright steamy."

"Will you stop that!"

He gave her an innocent, surprised look. "Stop what?"

"Stop...talking like that. All sexy and low."

He quirked a brow.

"Oh, forget it. You probably don't even know when you do it." The latch came free, and she pulled the strap away, then immediately started on his tie, giving it a good jerk first, making his head bounce in the sand. Before he could reprimand her, she said, "Ever since I've known you, you've done that. You're nothing more than walking testosterone, and while *some* women might like it, I do not."

She gave the tie another vicious jerk, loosening the knot, and he grabbed her hands. "Will you stop before you strangle me! Damn, woman, I was discussing the weather, and somehow you got on the topic of my hormones!"

Melanie jerked away and came awkwardly to her feet. She shoved her tangled hair out of her face and tried again to untwist her long, wet skirts. After a moment of futile effort, she gave up. Propping her hands on her hips, she said, "I brought it up because that's all you are! Male hormones waiting to burst." She threw her arms wide in apt description.

Adam slowly sat up and had his elbows resting on his bent knees, his head cocked to stare directly at her. "Is that right? Well, I'd say that puts you in something of a predicament then, doesn't it."

Warily, she asked, "What do you mean?"

"I hate to break it to you. No, actually I'm glad to break it to you. This little island appears to be deserted. We're all alone—just you, me, and my bursting hormones." He grinned wickedly. "For who knows how long?"

Frozen for three heartbeats, Melanie stared at him. Then she scoffed. "Don't be ridiculous."

"It's true." Adam stood, brushed off his muscled backside and looked around. "You weren't paying any attention, but when I first spotted the island we were still pretty far out. I could damn near see it from end to end, and not once did I see any sign of life. Not a kid, not a dog, not a single soul."

"You're just trying to scare me."

"Nope. The last thing I want is a hysterical woman on my hands." He peeled off his suit coat and shook it out, then tossed it onto a clump of dry, prickly-looking grass. He did the same with his shoes and socks. "I'm only hoping we'll be able to find some kind of food and water."

"Adam, stop it." She glared at him from under lowered brows. Her heart raced; her stomach felt queasy. "There are no deserted islands in Florida anymore. It's a tourist mecca. This is just your way of being mean again."

He took two quick steps to her and caught her chin in his hand. "I'm a grown man, damn it. I don't run around trying to frighten women or be mean. Do you honestly think anyone on that boat will notice us missing? Do you think they'll even know where to look for us? How long do you think it'll be before we're missed?"

The second he touched her, her tongue became useless. She couldn't muster up a single word or protest. Her heartbeat slowed; her breath caught.

Damn, she felt vulnerable! She'd so wanted to make an impression on him after she saw him on the boat. She'd been planning and plotting on when she'd introduce herself, what she'd say, how she'd say it to let him know without a single doubt that she would no longer be bothered by him, that she was a woman now, totally immune to him.

But then she'd gone overboard, and he'd done the unexpected and dove in after her. She thought of how she'd acted in the water and wanted to dig a hole in the sand to hide. Now here she was, insulting him, baiting him, reacting to him.

She jerked her chin away. "I'm sorry."

"What?"

"I… No one will notice me missing. I came alone and I wasn't exactly friendly to anyone on the boat."

"You came alone?"

Oh, why did he have to focus on that one small tidbit? She hadn't even meant to admit that much. She put her chin in the air and said, "Yes. Alone."

He looked her over slowly from head to toe, made a grunting sound, then turned away and started unbuttoning his shirt. "I figured you'd be married to some young yuppie executive type by now."

If all had gone as planned, she would have been. Thank God she'd called it off in time.

When Adam shrugged out of his shirt, at first all she could do was stare at his chest. Hard, lean, covered with a light dusting of hair a shade or two darker than his golden head, it was the type of chest female fantasies were made of. When his hands went to the buttons on his slacks, her mouth fell open, then snapped shut. In a croak, she asked, "What do you think you're doing?"

Without looking at her, he said, "You don't expect me to go exploring our little island in suit pants, do you?"

He didn't wait for an answer. The pants were shoved down, and she whirled around so fast her head swam. But she hadn't been quite quick enough. She saw snug cotton boxer briefs—wet briefs—molded closely to his lower body. The man was a total fiend.

"Adam," she said, doing her best to keep her tone calm and reasonable, "put your pants back on."

"No way. If you had any sense, you'd lose that skirt."

She clutched her skirts protectively to her body. "I will do no such thing!"

"Suit yourself. But I don't think it'll hold up long if you don't wash the salt water out of it and let it air dry."

He had a point, not that she intended to disrobe in front of him. It didn't matter that she wore matching shorts beneath the skirt and underwear under that. Her ex-fiancé had told her numerous times that she needed to put on weight, to gain some curves. And toward the end, she'd finally realized he didn't find her attractive at all. Oh, he put up a good front, and he tried. Jerry was always pleasant, mannerly, proper. That was one of the reasons she'd broken things off with him; he seemed more emotionless every day, like he had no depth, at least not where she was concerned.

She'd come here to rest, to get control of her emotions after the painful breakup. Ha! Controlling her emotions around Adam had always been impossible.

It was imperative she carry her own weight, that she prove to him her little display in the water was an aberration. She could and would fend for herself.

She was still figuring ways to do that when his warm breath touched the back of her neck. She hadn't even noticed him approaching!

"One thing hasn't changed, I see."

Melanie froze, not daring to move in case his mouth

actually touched her skin—in which case she knew she'd likely faint. Her every nerve ending felt stretched tight with him so close. Even her fingertips tingled. "What?"

"You're still a shy little thing."

But she wasn't shy. She was just…affected by him. She'd always been affected by him. He made her nervous and tongue-tied and loopy. From the first day she'd seen him, he'd look at her and her stomach would do flips. Forcing herself to turn, she had her mouth open with a scathing retort when she remembered his state of undress.

Oh, my. Her lips wouldn't move. As to that, neither would her eyes; they stayed glued on the bare, very male body he presented. Her imagination hadn't done him justice.

Adam chucked her chin. "Come on. We'll walk along the shore a bit and see if we can find any signs of habitation."

He moved away from her, and she stared, heart racing, as he sauntered to his bag and picked it up. He left his discarded clothes lying amid the long, dry grass. As he went past her again, he whistled a jaunty tune.

If she'd found a rock, she'd have thrown it at his head. Frustrated, annoyed and somewhat intrigued, Melanie hurried to catch up.

As Adam had said, many things had changed. But one thing that hadn't was his appeal. The man still had it in spades. And though she hated to admit it, she'd never been immune.

3

"IF YOU'RE SO SURE we're alone, why drag along your bag?"

Adam smiled slightly to himself. Though she did her best to be cavalier, her voice shook. Good. Let her fret awhile. Misery loved company, and his mind was so jumbled at the moment, it was filled with the worst kind of misery.

He'd missed his meeting. Hiding his reaction from Mel wasn't easy, but he had no intention of letting her know how important the deal had been for him. Not only that, but it had taken mere moments in her company for him to revert to form, to become the taunting bully she'd always claimed him to be. He hadn't treated a woman with less than full respect and gentleness since he'd moved away from Brockton.

Except for now. By word and attitude he'd proved Mel right, that he hadn't really changed at all. And it made him madder than hell. "I have important stuff inside. Where I go, it goes."

His dark boxers were nearly dry now, but her long skirt was still dripping. He wished she'd lose it. One nice long look at her legs would make his outlook brighter. She was still so slender, so fragile. Seven years hadn't changed that, but emotionally, she was more sturdy. He laughed. Hell, she was almost mean, as she'd accused him of being.

"Why are you laughing?"

He slanted her a look. "Private joke." But while he was looking at her, he noticed how fair her skin was. "You got sunscreen on?"

She looked at her body, then crossed her arms over the delicate skin of her midriff. "I did have. But that was before our little dip in the ocean."

"Damn. Much as I hate to do this…" He stopped and set his bag on the sand, then knelt before it. "I have a shirt you can put on. I don't want to see you get burned."

"Playing hero again?"

His jaw locked for a second as her words hit him. He was so far from heroic it was laughable. She knew it too, and probably used the term as more of an insult than a compliment. He surveyed her smug little expression, then shook his head. "No, I just don't want to hear you whining later if your tender skin gets pink."

"I do not whine."

"The hell you don't."

She started to stalk away and he called out, "Just where do you think you're going, honey? If you get lost and a wild boar gets you, it's no sweat off my nose."

She halted in her tracks, then slowly turned to him. "There are no wild boars on a Florida island."

Shoving clothes aside, he lifted out the much acclaimed guidebook and shook it at her. "Says different in here!" So far, he really had no idea what the damn manual said. He hadn't had a chance to look it over completely.

She stomped back to him, kicking up sand along the way. She had the attitude of a very tiny, very female bull. "Let me see that."

He held it behind his back. "I don't think so. It's

mine. In fact, I've got a lot of useful stuff here in my bag. Let's see—" He shoved the booklet under his backside so she couldn't get to it then began rummaging in his bag. "There's the shirt you could surely use to protect your delicate hide if only you'd stop being such a witch. Toothpaste and toothbrush. A few candy bars, gum, shampoo and soap. A razor." He looked at her and grinned his most evil grin. "Clean Skivvies and even a pack of condoms."

His evil grin was nothing compared to her aristocratic look of disdain. "Well, unless you intend to sweet-talk the boars, I seriously doubt you'll need the condoms."

"A smart man is always prepared."

"Then I'm so surprised you thought of it."

Her look was so snotty, he grinned, then actually laughed. "Damn, you're still a world-class snob."

She gasped at him. "I was *never* a snob!"

He held up one finger, interrupting her tirade. "But…you're a snob with nothing more than the clothes on your back. If you want to borrow anything I have, you better start being nice."

"Go to hell!"

He made an amused tsking sound. "Such language. Should I remind you, Mel, that there aren't any stores on a deserted island? Your charge cards won't do you much good."

"I don't even have my purse with me. Not that it matters, because we'll be rescued by dinnertime."

He shook his head in a pitying fashion. "You're still so naive."

"I was never a snob and I was never naive. You were always too busy provoking me to know me at all."

The words had a grain of truth, at least in regard to

their earlier relationship, before high school. But he'd be damned if he'd let her make him feel bad now. "I was provoking because you were such a snob."

Her face colored in silent rage. "And you're a pessimist. Keep all your precious belongings. I won't need them."

Adam considered her stance; hands on hips, her hair a dark, glossy halo around her head, her wispy, flowery skirt. The island served as the perfect backdrop for her. She looked exotic and desirable and damn sexy. "Wanna bet?"

"What?"

He pursed his lips. "I'll make you a deal. You'll get my sincere apology if we're rescued by dinner."

"And if we're not?"

"Well, now, let's see." His gaze focused on her mouth, and his voice dropped slightly. "I always wondered what it would be like to kiss you."

She gasped; her cheeks turned hot for an entirely different reason. "I don't believe you."

"Oh, it's true. I wondered about it. A lot."

"Well, you can just go on wondering!"

And he would, he had no doubt of that. Even the seven years they'd been separated hadn't been enough to obliterate the fantasies he had about her. But now here was a chance to live them, at least to some degree. "Chicken?"

Her eyes darkened, brows drew together. "Of course not."

He stepped closer, whispering, "Then bet me."

"Jerk."

"And here I thought I was your hero."

She made a soft, growling sound, then gave an

abrupt nod. "All right. But you'll be sorry when you lose."

"Will you be sorry, too?"

She turned her back on him. Smiling, Adam dug out the long-sleeved white dress shirt. Mel was stiff, nearly vibrating with anger. He should have been ashamed for taunting her, a gut reaction he thought he'd lost after high school, but instead, he was turned on. She seemed so sexy with her new outspoken manner.

"Here, let's get you covered up before you burn. It's the truth, I don't cotton to roasted woman. I'd rather kiss you tonight when you're not in pain from the sun." He tried his warmest, most sincere expression on her, the one that usually had women agreeing with his every word.

But when he reached to put the shirt on her, she stepped back and swallowed hard. "Adam, I don't think we should fight."

"Absolutely not." He reached for her again, and she caught his hand.

"In all seriousness, we could be stuck here for a few hours." Her expression was earnest, concerned.

"Could be." He wouldn't remind her again just how seriously they were stranded. Tonight, when he kissed her senseless, she'd finally accept the truth. The anticipation was almost enough to soften his disappointment over losing the deal. Almost.

"Could we call a truce?"

"Are you backing out of the bet?"

She sighed. "No."

"Then by all means, behold a peaceable man. Now put on the shirt." He slipped it around her, but he had to lean close to do so, and suddenly she gasped.

"Oh, my God! Your head."

He eyed her cautiously. "I know it hurts like the devil but it's still on my shoulders, isn't it?"

"You're bleeding!"

"Quit squawking, Mel. I'm fine. I just knocked my head on the slide when I went overboard."

"Here, sit down." She pushed at his shoulders and Adam stared at her, not budging. Her tiny hands and puny strength were easy to ignore. But her sudden concern... He wasn't quite sure what to think of it. Over the years he'd imagined many things from Mel, but never genuine concern.

"Mel..."

"Melanie," she corrected, but this time without heat. "Now sit."

No woman other than his mother had ever pampered him, except in bed, so he sat and awaited a unique experience. His manly ego, however, insisted that he protest one last time. "I'm fine, Mel, really."

She leaned over him, and he could feel her soft breath on his shoulder, could smell the woman sweet scent of her. Her slender fingers touched, oh so gently, his scalp.

In hushed, pained tones, she whispered, "You've got a terrible gash, Adam."

He decided a little sympathy from her wouldn't be a bad thing. As long as he was going to let her believe he'd jumped overboard after her, he might as well go for broke. Besides, he would have come to her rescue—if he hadn't fallen in by accident. "It's not still bleeding, is it?"

"A little."

"Well, see then? It's almost stopped, so there's nothing to worry about. And after all that time in the ocean, it's been cleaned out good."

She didn't sound convinced. "I took first-aid classes in college. I think we need to put some pressure on it."

"Mel, my head hurts enough as it is without you playing doctor." He heard what he said, knew she'd heard it too, and grinned. "Then again..."

"Just be quiet, Adam." As she spoke, she came around him and opened his bag. "You must have something in here we could use as a bandage and wrap."

He caught her hands and pulled them away. "Quit riffling through my things!"

"Stop being such a baby!"

"I'm not...." He hesitated, caught by the worry in her gaze, the near desperation. She truly wanted to help him. *Mel Tucker was showing him tenderness.*

That fact left him a little shaky. "Oh, hell, go ahead then. Suit yourself. I can see you're going to be stubborn about this."

The first thing she pulled out of his bag was his business envelope, thickly padded and sealed. It held the contract of buying terms, a check, insurance papers. Everything he'd needed for his future. Now all wasted.

"What's this?"

He stared at the blazing sun and silently cursed the ocean, the weather and drunk captains. "Pretty much useless garbage at this point."

His tone was mean enough to put off more questions.

Of course, that didn't stop Mel. The rich lived by their own rules and seldom let anything stand in their way.

Still rummaging, she said, "It looks important."

"*Was* important. But I missed the deadline by now."

"Deadline for what? Oh, look. These will do nicely as a bandage."

Appalled, Adam growled, "I'm damn well not wearing my underwear on my head!"

"Oh, for goodness sake, I'll rip them up. They're white cotton and will work perfectly."

He shook his head. "Hell, no."

"Adam…"

"If you're so set on underwear, let's use yours."

Her eyes widened, and she sputtered. "I'm wearing mine!"

"So take them off."

She looked ready to smack him. "Mine won't do."

"Why not? You said underwear was perfect and I'd damn sure rather it be—"

"Mine aren't white and they aren't cotton," she blurted, then he watched, fascinated, as her face turned bright red.

He was still cad enough to love seeing a woman's blush, especially Mel's. "Do tell."

She wouldn't look at him. "Stop trying to distract me."

"I was distracting myself." Not that it would take much with her standing there still damp, her skin dewy, her skirt and halter clinging to her body. She was as thin as she'd been in high school, her ribs visible below the halter top, but she looked so soft, too, so damn female.

He cleared his throat. "All right. We'll skip undies altogether. Find something else. This'll do." He lifted out a black T-shirt he'd brought for the trip home, to wear with his jeans. Once the business meeting ended, he'd planned to get comfortable again. He positively hated suits.

Mel shook her head. "Black isn't good because it'll be harder to see if you're still bleeding."

"It's either this or your panties. Take your pick."

She took the T-shirt. "You always were a rotten bully, Adam Stone."

"So you ought to be used to it, right?" He was done trying to convince her he'd changed. What difference did it make, anyway? When all was said and done, they were still separated by a background that would never alter.

Adam drew his key ring from his bag. It had a small but lethally sharp pocketknife attached. He attacked the shirt with a vengeance.

Staring at the knife, Mel asked, "Why in the world are you carrying that?"

"Old instincts are hard to shake. I got the knife when I was sixteen, when we still lived by the river." He glanced at her, saw her appalled expression and shook his head. "I've never gutted anyone, honey. I've just kept it for protection. And because now I'm used to carrying it."

"Good grief, do you still have your leather jacket, too?"

He grinned. "As a matter of fact, yeah, I do. But it's too small for me to wear anymore. My mother bought me that jacket by taking in sewing. It means a hell of a lot to me. Of course, if she'd known what a redneck I felt like wearing it, she probably would have taken it back."

She laughed. "You did have your moments of mischief."

Adam tipped his head and studied her. "What about you?"

"What about me?"

He tweaked a dark, glossy curl by her ear. "You still got those Minnie Mouse combs you used to wear in your hair, one on each side?"

She looked surprised that he remembered; he could have told her there was little he'd ever forgotten, at least about her. He remembered the cute little dresses she used to wear, how serious she always looked, how alone.

His heart twisted in a familiar pang, and he cleared his throat. He didn't have the material things she'd had, but he'd had a close group of friends and always knew his family was there to give him as much moral support as he needed. "Do you still have them?"

She dipped her head to hide her face. "I do. I bought them myself when I turned fourteen. My mother thought they were frivolous, but I always loved them."

"Worth a lot, huh?"

"Worth a lot to me, but not to too many other people."

Adam felt like they were suddenly on dangerous ground. He knew Melanie had never had the best relationship with her parents. They'd loved her, there was never any doubt of that. But their expectations had always been pretty high. She wasn't allowed to be a regular kid, with regular faults. She was supposed to be better than that. Maybe those silly little combs had been her first attempt at independence.

Adam abruptly changed the subject. He didn't like seeing her so melancholy. He'd take her temper any day. "So what are we doing here? Do you want to use this damn shirt or not? Or are you just waiting for me to bleed to death."

"You said you weren't bleeding that much any more!"

He shrugged, which only annoyed her more. He handed her the sliced-up T-shirt, then suffered through her efforts.

Actually *suffer* was a very apt word. Despite her new pique, she didn't hurt him. But she was so gentle when she cleaned away the rest of the sand and smoothed his hair, when she held the wadded bandage in place then wrapped a strip of the shirt around his forehead like a headband. Her scent enveloped him again, and twice he felt her breasts brush his shoulder.

Oh, hell. He was wearing no more than snug boxers, and his interest would be blatantly obvious if he didn't distract himself and quick.

"So what were you doing on this trip, all alone? Very few people vacation without a companion."

She carefully knotted the wrap. With a shrug in her tone, she said, "I'm used to being alone. And it makes it easier for me to think."

"To think about what?"

She finished with his bandage and sat back on her heels. The skirt pulled tight over her long thighs and smooth knees. That held his attention for several heartbeats, and when he finally looked at her face, he decided she looked uncertain. Adam thought she'd refuse to answer, but she lifted one shoulder and said, "About what to do with myself for the rest of my life."

"You couldn't figure that out back in Brockton?" Adam closed his bag and stood.

She stood also and dusted the sand off herself. "There were...distractions at home."

He took her hand with his free one and started them down the beach again. Mel didn't object, and he enjoyed touching her. Her fingers were so slender, her hand so tiny in his large one. "What kind of distractions?"

"Oh, family, friends…an ex-fiancé."

That last distraction caused his stomach to tighten. Trying to sound only mildly interested, he asked, "Family?"

"Surely you remember my mother and father. They're a bit…overwhelming. And they like to try to run my life."

"I remember they did run your life. They pretty much chose your friends, your clothes, your first car."

She nodded. "But that was before college. I came back a different woman."

She looked at him, and he could tell his reaction mattered to her. He smiled. "If what I've seen so far is evidence, I'd say you're very different."

"Yes." She let out a breath, satisfied. "But they didn't like it much. They're constantly trying to make my decisions for me, especially about who I marry. I needed time away from their campaigning."

"What about your friends?"

"They mean well, but they don't understand."

"Understand what?"

"Me." They walked several yards before she added, "They thought I should go back to my fiancé, that we'd make a perfect couple. Jerry is well established, influential. They all thought he worshiped me, but…"

Again his stomach clenched and his heart thumped awkwardly. The man she described was everything Adam would never be, the perfect cultured mate for a woman of her breeding. Adam had always known when Mel married, it would be to someone exactly like that.

He'd hated it then, and he hated it now.

The rain had stopped, but the humidity was almost choking. He felt he couldn't get a deep enough breath. "So what happened?"

"I didn't love him. And he didn't love me."

A warmth surged through Adam, making his muscles ripple. He clenched her hand a little tighter. "Your parents and your friends don't think love matters?"

"They thought I'd grow to love him."

She looked out over the ocean, avoiding his gaze. But Adam didn't mind. Just seeing her profile was nice. He liked the upward tilt of her nose, the way her long lashes cast shadows over her cheeks. He even liked her ears.

Damn. "Do you think it's possible you would have?"

Blue eyes darted his way, incredulous. "No. Not ever."

"Then you made the right decision."

"I know. But now what?" With her toes pointed, she kicked up sand and swung his hand just a little. "I mean, I need to find a job of some sort and get my life together."

Frowning, Adam asked, "You need to find work?"

Her eyes widened. "Oh! I don't mean that I'm broke or anything like that. But you see, Jerry is a lawyer, and I was his secretary. After I broke my engagement, it didn't seem right to work for him. And I wanted to do something new, anyway. Besides, work shouldn't only be about money."

Adam shook his head in disbelief. "Only the rich could have such an attitude."

"That's not true." She frowned at him. "Don't you want to enjoy your work? To have goals to reach for and take pride in? Don't you want to make a difference somehow?"

"I wanted to make a difference to my mother. She deserves some peace now, some time to take it easy. And I wanted to give my brother a chance, lots of chances, to do the things I didn't get to do."

Very tentatively, she asked, "You say all that as if it's impossible now."

"No. I'll get to that point eventually. But it should have been today." He released her hand to run his fingers through his hair, only to encounter the makeshift bandage. His fist dropped to thump against his bare thigh. "If I hadn't gone overboard, I'd be on Marco Island right now, buying a small resort. My mother and Kyle are probably sitting by the phone, waiting for my call this very minute."

"Adam…"

He heard her concern but couldn't bear it if she felt sorry for him. He shook his head, dredging up lost control. "Forget it, Mel."

"But if you have the money to buy one resort, then surely you could just get another."

He laughed at her, more aware than ever of the differences in their outlooks. "This particular resort was dirt cheap because it needs a lot of work that Kyle and I could have done after it was ours. Unlike you or your family, I'm well used to working up a sweat. I could have turned the resort around. But the agent, Mr. Danvers, was clear that if I missed the deadline, it would be sold to the next bidder, who was only slightly below me. I scrambled around for two weeks getting things in order—only to fall off the goddamned boat."

Adam abruptly shut his mouth, disgusted with the situation and with himself. Why had he opened up to her like that? The details of his real estate deal were none of her business. Hell, he'd wanted to impress her, not drive home how shaky his financial position still was.

"Tell me about your family, Adam."

He scrubbed at his face, then twisted to see her. She knelt in the sand beside him, her expression sincere, curious. Adam shrugged. "Kyle is totally different from me, more like my mother. He smiles all the time, and nothing gets him down. When we were younger, and things got rough at home, I'd always end up in trouble, fighting with someone or mouthing off at school. Not Kyle. Everyone likes him."

"And your mother?"

"She's the strongest person I know." His eyes narrowed and he looked out at the endless expanse of sea. "Even when Dad died, she held up, doing what had to be done, getting through each day. As soon as I could make enough money, I moved them away from Brockton, so we could all have a new start. We didn't go far, even stayed in Ohio, but now they were looking forward to Florida." His jaw tightened and he threw a fistful of sand. "Damn, I hate to let them down."

Mel's hand touched his, and she whispered, "I'm sorry."

Her soft apology made him realize what a heel he'd been. It wasn't her fault he'd lost his balance, but he let her believe he'd jumped in to rescue her. Oh, hell.

"I fell in, Mel."

She touched his shoulder. "I know. Trying to save me."

He glared at her over his shoulder. "Didn't you hear me? I *fell* in. Yes, I made a grab for you, but no, I did not leap in to rescue you. Hell, that would have been an idiotic thing to do. If I hadn't lost my balance I would have just told the captain to turn the stupid boat around."

She looked confused. "You lied to me?"

"No, I didn't lie. You just assumed."

"And you didn't correct me!"

Shrugging, he said, "You were so anxious to…comfort me. I didn't want to miss the experience."

She fumed in impotent silence for three seconds, then kicked sand at him and stalked off.

"A repeat performance, Mel!" he shouted to her retreating back. "You keep playing the same scene—get mad and walk away. Only here, there's no place to walk to."

"Go to hell," she yelled without turning.

She took off at a furious trot, and she was nearly out of sight around a cove heavy with mangrove trees when Adam decided he'd have to apologize "Mel? Come on, Mel, wait up."

No answer. Grabbing his bag, he headed after her, calling her name. "Mel!"

The sun hung low in the sky, a heavy red ball turning the water in the cove crimson with its reflection.

He picked up his pace, his injured head pounding with every step, then almost ran into her when he rounded the bend she'd taken. "Damn it, you could have…"

His words dropped off. Ahead of them, some hundred yards up the beach, was a house. Well, sort of a house, more like a ratty shack. It was almost in the ocean because of the eroded shoreline. Exposed pilings beneath the structure showed how precariously it stood, and to Adam's mind exemplified the seriousness of their situation. If folks were anywhere about, they would have knocked such a dangerous eyesore down. Oh, they were stranded, all right. He wondered how often, if ever, people visited this damn island.

He took a step forward just as Mel took one back, closer to his side. "Do you think anyone is around?" she asked in a whisper, and he realized she was nervous. And in being nervous, she'd automatically come to him. The man.

He felt like Tarzan, ready to defend her against all predators. He wasn't rich, but for now, he was all she had. He grinned with the image. "Come on. Let's go exploring."

He led her to the front door of the house, but the steps were broken and separated from the main structure by the shift of the land. He set his bag on the sand and said in his best macho voice, "You probably should wait here."

"Adam, be careful." She fretted behind him, twisting her hands. "You don't know what could be inside there."

Wild boars? He grinned and glanced at her while shoving the door open—and got bombarded by a flurry of large flying insects.

Startled, Adam yelled, then fell backward into the sand, hitting his head once again.

4

MELANIE RAN HALFWAY down the beach before she realized what a coward she'd been. The bugs, giant roaches of some kind, were gone, their dark cloud moving far away.

Adam still lay where he'd landed, and she grew immediately concerned. She sprinted toward him. "Adam!" She came to a rushing halt beside his prone body, accidentally kicking sand over his chest and shoulders. He looked like a downed warrior in his headband and dark, snug underwear, with the rest of his magnificent, tanned body bare. She took a moment to observe him unaware, grew even more breathless, then shook herself.

Her pulse racing at Mach speed, she knelt gingerly beside him. "Adam?

He groaned.

Her heart seemed to drop to the pit of her stomach. "Oh, thank God. Are you all right?" She cradled his head on her lap and touched his jaw. "Adam, can you answer me?"

He cocked one eye open, stared at her breast near to his face and closed his eye again. "Nice, Mel, real nice."

"Adam," she warned.

"No, don't slug me. There's already a rusty marching band playing on my brain." He sighed, then added, "Oh, hell, I feel like a fool."

Stroking his jaw and chin, she asked, "Why?"

"It was just a few bugs, Mel."

"Ha! They were giant cockroach-looking bugs, and I almost fainted!"

"Yeah, well, having grown up by the river, I've seen plenty of bugs."

She shuddered. "Not me."

"I know." He made a smirking face, as if it was a crime not to have lived with bugs. Then he added, "But don't pass out on me here, because I'm not up to lugging your dead weight up and down this damn beach."

Only the very real pain she could see in his eyes kept her from dumping his head off her lap. That, and the picture in her mind of where Adam had lived. Once, when she'd been around sixteen, she'd snuck down by the river to spy on him. Driven by some inner demon, she'd wanted to look at him, to see him. He'd been especially provoking that day, and she'd had some far-fetched idea of finding out more about him so she'd be better prepared to deal with him.

She'd gotten the shock of her life.

The outside of the trailer had been as tidy as anyone could make it, almost hiding the fact that it was falling apart. Wildflowers had been planted around the skirt of the trailer in an attempt to hide holes. Melanie, in her misconceptions of the world, had wondered why they didn't move. It wasn't long after that she found out Adam's father had cancer, causing him to miss more and more work.

Some of the area residents had taken up a collection for the family, and she still remembered feeling ashamed when her parents donated so little, when she'd wanted to give so much.

It was no wonder he'd always resented her.

To hide her sudden discomfort and the pity she still felt, she quipped, "You know something, Stone? You've got worse mood swings than my mother when she went through menopause. And frankly, she was a royal bitch."

He chuckled. "That bad, huh? Well, considering I missed the most important meeting of my life, I spent an hour in the ocean using muscles I'd forgotten I had, my brains have been scrambled twice now, and I'm presently in a position I've fantasized over but can't do a damn thing about, then I'd say I'm justified."

Melanie's heart gave an excited stumble over his words. What had he fantasized? Certainly not about her. He'd never shown her anything but disdain. Sure, today he'd joked about kissing her, but that was just his way of making her uncomfortable. Yet the way he'd said it while eyeing her breasts…

Carefully, measuring every word, she said, "I can easily take care of your missed meeting, your muscles look…unforgettable to me, your head will feel better soon. Oh, and what did you fantasize about?"

Her nonchalance didn't fool him. He slowly sat up to face her, his large body too close, his gaze too intent on her face. She felt herself blushing without knowing why.

He worked his jaw in thought, then said, "I don't need you to do a damned thing about the missed meeting, so forget that. But I am glad you noticed my muscles—especially since I've more than noticed your soft little body. My head is going to fall off my shoulders long before it stops aching." He touched her cheek, the line of her jaw. "And you," he whispered. "I've fantasized about you, Mel, about touching you, kissing you." He leaned closer, his mouth only an inch away from hers. "Those last few years all I could think about was how damned exciting it would be to get you under me."

Oh, wow. Her vision clouded, and she had to part her lips to breathe. The heat wasn't only surrounding her now, it was inside her, a part of her. No man had ever talked to her this way, not even Jerry, and she'd been engaged to him. It was exhilarating and stimulating and...this was Adam. She narrowed her gaze.

"Are you trying to humiliate me again?"

He drew back just a bit and stared at her. "Again?"

"Like in high school, when you asked me out. Oh, don't look so innocent! I know what would have happened if I'd been dumb enough to say yes. You'd have laughed and told everyone what a fool I was. That's the only reason you asked me in the first place, isn't it?"

He looked equal parts frustrated, angry and hot. "I asked you out because I wanted to."

"Oh, sure. And that's why you suggested we go driving instead of to a school dance or the movies where someone might have seen us."

"You're the one who would have cared, Mel. My reputation was already shot. Folks saw me as dirt poor, no-account, and a troublemaker."

"You were a troublemaker."

He ignored that little truism. "And you were the town princess, too good for the humble masses. Hell, your mommy and daddy had nothing but contempt for the rest of us, and they would have had me shot if they knew I'd asked you out." He shrugged, looking awkward for just a moment. "I figured you might go if no one would ever know about it."

She stared at him, appalled at his perceptions, feeling sick deep inside herself. He was right in predicting her parents' reactions. They wouldn't have been pleased. But to think of Adam as sincerely wanting to date her... Well, that would take a major attitude adjustment. He'd been so cocky back then, as if he'd been unaware of his poverty, of his social circumstances. He'd always seemed so self-contained, unaffected by others, especially by her.

Could he have felt as vulnerable as she did?

"Why?" She asked it simply, the question uppermost in her mind. "Why would you have wanted to go out with me?"

His expression became almost ruthless. With the black headband wrapped around his fair hair, his bare shoulders glistening in the hot evening sun, he looked like a savage.

His golden eyes glittered with intent, and then without a word he grabbed her by the back of the neck, pulled her closer and pressed his mouth to hers.

For a mere second he was still, the pressure firm. They both seemed frozen, afraid to move. Then he groaned and twisted and gathered her closer, his mouth opening, devouring. She felt the hot stroke of his tongue, urgent and deep, the sharp touch of his teeth, and she gave a small groan of her own.

His arms closed around her, bringing her as near as he could get her. Everything about him seemed to be hot and hard, like a steel inferno. Pressed against his damp chest, she felt every ragged breath he drew.

Being alone with Adam like this, hearing the things he claimed, was a fantasy come to life. As a young woman, she'd built a world around the idea of luring in the irresistible Adam Stone. Everything about him had excited her, and compared to him, other men had seemed lacking—including her fiancé. "Adam—"

His teeth nipped her earlobe and made her gasp. "Sh," he whispered, barely breathing the word so that all the fine hairs on her body stood at titillated attention. Her body felt ripe, hungry.

"Tell me that you want me, too, Mel."

Oh, she did. She really did. "We…we need to talk, Adam."

He leaned back to give her a warm smile, his gaze searching, pleased. "But you're not denying you want me."

She started to, only the words wouldn't come out, not with him looking at her that way. His hands stayed busy, slowly pushing the white shirt open and brushing over the exposed skin of her shoulders, arms and throat as if he couldn't quite touch her enough. Everywhere his fingers trailed, she felt gooseflesh rise, making her more sensitive. He appeared almost reverent, his gaze so hot she felt the touch of it against her skin.

She'd secretly dreamed of being with him like this, and she wanted so badly to give in. But she knew she'd caused him a lot of grief, and first she had to remedy that. She leaned away from the temptation he offered. "I want to buy the resort, Adam. I owe it to you."

Very slowly, he released her. His expression was cold, blank. "There was a bidder right behind me."

"So I'll make him an offer he can't refuse."

He jerked to his feet, then stared at her. "I don't want your charity, Mel."

"Charity?"

"I don't live on the riverbank anymore. I can damn well take care of myself, without your interference."

His attitude stunned her. "You're being unreasonable, Adam. I can afford to do this—"

"And I can't. Just like old times, huh?"

They stared at each other in heavy silence. He was so distant, so sarcastic, it was as if the delicious kiss had never happened. Melanie bit her lip to keep her emotions in check. His feelings were plain, but then, so were hers. She knew what she needed to do, she just didn't know how Adam would react. "You're a bull-headed jerk, Adam Stone."

He turned away to observe the shoreline. After several more seconds, he said, "It's going to be dark soon. We should finish checking out the house to see if there's anything in there we can use."

The setting sun cast everything in shadow, lending an eerie quality to the island. Adam disappeared behind the house, and she didn't bother to follow him. How had everything changed so suddenly?

"I've found us some food."

She stared at him, carefully hiding her hurt. He held out two withered oranges.

"Behind the house." He watched her as he spoke, and she had the feeling he was trying to gauge her mood. "The orange tree isn't much to brag on, but next to that is a palm tree loaded with coconuts. We won't starve."

Fighting with him wouldn't solve anything, so she tried for a look of enthusiasm. "I can live with fruit."

He looked relieved, and even smiled at her. "They were probably planted by whoever used to live here. According to the guidebook, citrus trees are usually only on the mainland. There's even a wild strawberry patch here, though it looks like the bugs have gotten to most of them. And some thorny blackberries."

He dropped the fruit in the sand by her feet, then went around to lever himself into the front door again. Watching Adam climb wearing no more than form-fitting Skivvies was a unique experience. Muscles and tendons flexed and pulled tight across his back and shoulders. His thighs were long, athletic. She crept closer to the house to peek inside.

It had obviously been no more than a functional fishing cabin. There were no separate rooms, just a few dividing walls. At the back of the house were an old porcelain tub and toilet, a broken mirror still on the wall. Various broken tools, dishes and garbage littered the inside.

"It's not exactly cozy."

Adam snorted. "If it rains again, and it will, at least we'll be able to keep dry. And I think I might be able to drag that tub outside to collect the rainwater."

The tub was dirty, chipped and rusted. "Pray, for what?"

"To drink and bathe, sweetheart. Unfortunately, there's no catering service here, no ice machine right around the corner, no hot showers. Or haven't you accepted yet that we're stuck here?"

She really wanted to smack him. "We'll be rescued soon."

"Dream on." He began heaving at the tub. A large slithery snake glided from beneath and slipped across the dusty floor to disappear into a crack between the wall and the baseboard. It moved so quickly, neither of them had time to react. Adam turned to her, one brow raised, and she quickly ducked out of sight.

Sometimes, she thought, life was hardly fair. She'd come on this stupid trip to get away from meddling friends and family, stress and pressure. She'd wanted peace and quiet, but instead she'd gotten stranded on a damn bug-and-snake infested island with the one man who'd always made her crazy. Now it seemed that so many things she'd thought about Adam were wrong, but it didn't matter, because he still despised her inherited wealth.

"Come here and give me a hand."

Melanie turned, saw Adam struggling to lower the tub to the ground through the open doorway and applauded. "Bravo, Stone. Anything else I can do for you?"

He mumbled something she didn't hear and let the tub drop with a thud. After jumping off the doorstep, he dragged the tub straight past her and right into the ocean.

"Adam! What are you doing?" She envisioned him climbing inside the tub and somehow sailing away—without her.

But the tub immediately sank, and he only went out knee deep, just enough to swish the salty sea water inside it.

"I'm washing it. Something's been nesting inside it."

Shuddering in distaste, Melanie stood fretfully just outside the touch of the foaming tide and watched, praying no sharks would eat Adam, because she really didn't think she could stand being stranded alone.

But when he waded out and she saw that his snug boxer briefs were once again soaked and clinging to his very male body parts, she began to wonder if being stranded alone might be safer than being with Adam Stone.

THE SUN WAS NEARLY down, the air cooler, and Adam felt ready to burn up. On every imaginable level, he was painfully aware of Melanie. He could smell her warm, female scent, could hear her occasional movement, feel the touch of her gaze on his body. In a burst of frustration, he growled, "Stop ogling me."

Affronted, Melanie exclaimed, "I'm not!"

"Ha." He wanted an argument, a way to vent. When he'd kissed her, he'd nearly lost his mind, she tasted so good. He'd wanted nothing more than to lay her down in the sand and make love to her. Then she'd offered him money, and he'd gone cold inside. She couldn't know what it was like to take charity, to be dependent on others to get by. But he knew. And that was one more major difference between them.

She had spunk, he'd give her that. Most women would be carping and crying and complaining right about now. Their prospects for the coming night did not look good. But not Mel. No, she didn't complain, she just went on insisting everything was dandy in that damn annoying Pollyanna way she had of looking at everything. Even with bedraggled clothes and ruined makeup, she managed to appear regal and in control. She sat before him, her legs crossed just so, her shoulders straight.

She was staring at him again.

"Damn it, Mel." He dropped to his knees in front of her, at the end of his control. "Do you want me to pick up where we left off?"

She looked at his mouth, then slowly shook her head. "I want to talk to you."

"That again?" He plopped down, feeling the gritty sand on the back of his thighs, his palms. Damn sand everywhere. "All right. Let's get it over with."

She drew her knees up to her chest and carefully arranged her skirt over them. "Whether you deliberately jumped in to save me or not, the result was the same. You did get me to dry land, and I do owe you."

"That attitude ought to at least make our stay here interesting."

She drew a deep breath, and he had the feeling she was reaching for calm. "I intend to buy your resort, whether you like it or not."

He eyed her militant expression and shook his head. "No. Now would you like to wash all that paint off your face? It's pretty much a mess."

"Oh." She pressed her palms to her cheeks and looked a little embarrassed. He hoped that would be the end of it, that she'd get sidetracked with appearances and quit poking holes in his self-esteem.

Not Mel.

"I can wash up later."

"Not unless it rains again tonight. Already the puddles of fresh water are starting to disappear."

She blinked slowly, as if barely comprehending his words. "You expect me to wash my face in a puddle?"

"Well, honey, your options are somewhat limited right about now. It's either salt water, which is pretty sticky when it's drying, or a fresh rainwater puddle. The sand is clean, so the water is, too. And I can even loan you some of my soap—for a fee."

In the fading light, her pale blue eyes looked almost iridescent. He'd always thought she had the sexiest and most expressive eyes he'd ever seen. She didn't need makeup.

"What fee?"

"Another kiss, that's all." He could still taste her, and he wanted more.

"Bargaining away your goods? A real gentleman would just share."

"But we both know there's no real gentlemen on this island, don't we?" Provoking her seemed his only defense. If she was mad, she wouldn't talk about owing him. "Now what'll it be? You want the soap or not?"

Indignation made her eyes bright. "Oh, all right." Taking him by surprise, she leaned forward, grabbed his face in both hands and gave him a hard, dry smooch. He didn't even have time to pucker. "There. Now where's the soap?"

"That's it?" He had to fight to keep from laughing. Her averted gaze told him what that impromptu kiss had cost her in the way of nerve.

"That's it." She tried to look smug, but she avoided his gaze so the effect was minimal. "You didn't say what kind of kiss."

"I see I'll have to word myself more carefully in the future." Still smiling, Adam dug through his bag and pulled out the scented bar of green soap. It smelled like Brut cologne.

Melanie stared at it. "Is that all you have?"

"Sorry, but I didn't take into account feminine bathing preferences when packing it. It'll do the job. And you better hurry up before all the water either evaporates or sinks into the ground."

She took the soap and moved only a few feet away to where a shallow puddle had formed in the sand between some scrub grass and a young mangrove tree. On her knees, she bent forward and splashed her face. The position put her shapely rump up in the air, and Adam had to choke back several comments that tripped to the tip of his tongue.

Worse than that, he had to sit on his hands to keep from touching that sweet little bottom. He'd felt its softness when they were swimming to shore, had twice rested his head against her delicious buttocks. He'd had to fight the inclination to explore that area further while the opportunity presented itself. He'd even considered taking a few small nibbles, he'd always had a certain fondness for feminine posteriors, and everything about Melanie Tucker had always been a source of fascination.

She'd been too frightened of the ocean to notice his interest; he doubted that was the case now. But the woman obviously had no idea of her own charms. If she did, she sure wouldn't offer up such an irresistible temptation.

Hadn't her fiancé ever told her what a great bottom she had?

When she lingered, splashing again and again, he finally turned away. He wasn't into torture, and tonight his control seemed precarious, at best.

A few minutes later, face freshly scrubbed and even more appealing, Mel returned his soap to him. She sat beside him, looking more self-conscious than ever, but also a lot more determined. "Now, about the resort."

"Do you want a comb or some lotion?"

"Does the lotion smell like the soap?"

He grinned. "Sure does."

She stuck out her small hand, palm up.

Adam held the bottle out of reach. "You know you'll owe me again, only this time it'll be my choice."

She sighed. "And what exactly would your choice be?"

After looking her over from head to toe, he locked onto her gaze. Her eyes were wide and wary, and he thought he might be content to simply look at her all night. "It's a warm evening."

"Yes."

"I don't relish sleeping on this sand." He picked up a handful and let it sift through his fingers. "It sure as hell won't be very comfortable."

"We'll be rescued before it's a problem."

He grunted. Damn persistent witch. "Maybe, but if we're not, I want you to lose the skirt."

Her back snapped straight, and she glared at him. "This time you have to be joking."

"Nope." He enjoyed watching the flush bloom over her face and upper chest. He imagined her breasts rosy and warm, and shifted uncomfortably. "It's the only piece of material we have that's big enough to serve as a sheet. We can both snuggle up on it." When she looked furious, he asked softly, "What's the matter, Mel? If you're so sure we'll get rescued, then it won't be a problem."

He'd caught her and he knew it. His motives were twofold. If he could keep her mind on sex and off his personal business, she'd likely forget his financial confession. At the same time, he knew he'd gladly be stranded for a month if it meant he could fulfill his fantasy of being with her. Like an obsession that wouldn't go away, he wanted her as much now as he ever had. Maybe more, because he'd kissed her and knew how good she tasted, how perfect it had felt.

They had a staring contest going, one he knew he'd win because he enjoyed looking into her blue eyes.

"Oh, all right. But you're being outrageous and making me dislike you immensely."

He shrugged. "You've always disliked me. Not surprising. We're from different worlds."

Her mouth tightened. "I disliked you, Adam, not because you didn't have as much money as me. But because you were as provoking then as you are now."

Without a word, he handed her the lotion.

If she only knew how difficult it was for him to smell his favorite scent on her. It felt as if he'd branded her somehow, made her his by giving her his scent. It turned him on.

The entire atmosphere of the island was conducive to primal needs, reducing a man to his basic instincts. He wanted to protect her, provide for her. He wanted to claim her as his own in the most elemental way.

Damn, the coming night would be torture.

He was looking forward to it already.

5

THEY HAD FRUIT for dinner, but Melanie could barely eat as she watched the island grow darker and darker. Nervousness set in whenever she thought of the night to come, of being alone with Adam on a deserted island.

After cracking a couple of coconuts open and using his knife to slice up several oranges, he'd gone back up the beach to fetch the clothes he'd left behind and the raft they'd floated in on. Adam made the decision that they should stay by the house in case it rained again, but for now, they remained outside.

The heat had settled in like a damp blanket. A slight, balmy breeze barely stirred the air, rustling the dry grasses and fringed palm leaves. She got to her feet to gather the remains of their meal and put the scraps out of the way in a tidy pile. She knew Adam watched her every move, could feel his hot gaze touching on her everywhere. Earlier, before the sun had gone, he'd entertained himself by perusing his damn *Key to the Keys*, where he'd found the idea for scraping the coconut shells clean and filling them with the remains of the rainwater.

She bent to rinse her hands in one of the few remaining puddles and nearly jumped out of her skin when he shifted.

"Mel."

She slowly closed her eyes at the husky way he'd

said her name. She swallowed hard, then whispered, "Yes?"

A long moment of silence had her nerves pulled taut, when he finally said, "Come here."

With her back still to him, she sat on her heels, trying to calm her racing heart. Never had she been so conscious of another human being, but she should have suspected it would be this way. Good or bad, she'd always held a fascinated awareness of Adam that wouldn't go away, not even with the passing of seven years.

She was a grown woman, free to do as she pleased, and though she'd never really believed in casual sex, situations like this one just didn't happen often. And in truth, there was nothing casual in what she felt for Adam.

She turned her head to look at him. "Why?"

Lazily, his voice nearly drugged, he said, "You're keyed up. I can feel it. Come here and I'll comb your hair."

She lifted one hand to her tangled curls. That's all he wanted to do? He leaned against a palm tree, looking utterly relaxed, but she could feel his tension washing over her in waves. Her heartbeat doubled. "I...I can do it."

"I want to do it for you." When she started to protest, he said, "It's the price for using the comb. Now come here."

On legs that felt much too wobbly, she stood and walked to him until only a foot was between them. Adam took her hand, turned her around, then tugged her down between his thighs. Taking his time, he situated her just so. Melanie stared straight ahead at the silhouette of a palm tree against the dark gray sky.

Adam's breath touched her neck when he whispered, "Relax, Mel. I won't hurt you. Ever."

She had no response to that. Her senses rioted, her mind numb against everything but the feel of his fingers in her hair, gently untangling every curl.

"I like your hair short."

Conversation. Innocuous, innocent conversation. She grasped it like a lifeline, trying to hide the mixed jumble of emotions she suffered. "I cut it after college. Jerry didn't like it. He thought it looked too unruly."

The comb stilled for the slightest moment, then Adam laid it aside. "You always had beautiful hair. I remember when you went from braids to barrettes to those pretty combs. I used to imagine your hair trailing over my chest."

"Adam..."

"And my stomach."

She bit her lip, the imagery crystal clear in her mind.

"Jerry must have been a damn fool."

Her heart was already racing when the weight of Adam's hands settled on her shoulders. "It's getting late."

Not knowing what to say to that, she simply nodded.

"No one's coming tonight to rescue us, honey."

She nodded again. Even if a rescue crew tried, finding them in the darkness would be nearly impossible.

"We had a deal."

There it was—the thing she had dreaded most, and yet strangely hungered for. At least it was dark enough that he wouldn't be able to see her clearly. She knew what she looked like, knew she was too thin, too gangly. A man like Adam, who'd had more than his fair share of feminine attention, might very well be disappointed. The thought made her stomach churn.

He stood and pulled her up with him, then stepped in front of her. Heat seemed to pour off him in waves, bringing with it his heady scent—not of the now familiar cologne, but of the man. Breathing deeply, she drew that scent into herself. She felt drunk with the pleasure and nervousness of the moment.

"Mel?" He touched her cheek, smoothed his hand over her skin. "It's okay, honey."

She nearly collapsed. He wasn't going to pressure her. It was still her choice, and for that reason more than any other, she wanted to prove herself. She'd made a deal and she would stick to it. But when her fingers went to the tie at her skirt, he brushed her hands away and did the unwrapping himself, gently easing the knot apart and revealing her with slow anticipation as if she were a long-awaited gift.

Holding the skirt open with clenched fists, Adam simply looked. Melanie was grateful for the added shadows of the trees behind them, but then Adam dropped the skirt and took her hand, easing her into the moonlight. She held her breath, keeping her head high, refusing to show her uncertainty. She locked her thighs and waited.

For long, agonizing moments, he stood there, saying nothing, barely breathing. When she saw the beginning of his slow smile, she almost crumbled inside. "Don't...don't you *dare* laugh at me, Adam Stone."

His eyes glittered in the darkness, and his hands cupped her hips, gently squeezing. "Honey, I'm so far from laughing right now, I couldn't even work up a chuckle." He gave her a light, barely there kiss on her lips, then dropped to his knees in front of her.

Alarmed, she started to step back, but he held onto her.

"This has been coming a long time, Mel." His fingers on her hips flexed, caressing her. "Damn, I've wanted you so long, I can't remember when I haven't wanted you."

"You...you didn't even *like* me."

"I liked you too much."

Not giving her time to mull that stark confession over, he slid his hot palms up and down the backs of her thighs. He made her knees weak, her stomach jumpy. "You're perfect, Mel. Sleek and sexy." He glanced up at her, his expression fixed. "How the hell did you disguise yourself so well?"

He evidently didn't want an answer. He leaned forward and placed a warm, damp kiss on her navel. Stunned, she braced her hands on his shoulders and drew in a shaky breath. "Adam, I feel...funny." She could barely get the words out around the tightness in her throat.

"It's the coconut," he whispered, nibbling on her belly with his lips and rubbing his cheek against her. "It's an aphrodisiac."

"Don't...don't be ridiculous." She moaned when his hands glided higher, coasting over her bottom, then gripping her tight, pulling her closer to his kiss. His tongue dipped into her navel.

"True," he countered, concentrating his kisses over the low-riding waistband of her silky tap pants, "it's in the guidebook."

"Adam..."

"Aren't you turned on just a little, Mel?"

Oh, yes. But what she felt had nothing to do with coconut and everything to do with Adam Stone. It seemed he knew exactly how to touch her, where to kiss her, how to make her frantic with need. She'd pictured being with Adam many times, but she'd never imagined anything quite this intense.

Grasping her waist, he lowered her slowly, trailing kisses up her body as she sank onto her knees in the sand. His mouth lingered at her midriff; his tongue licked a hot path from rib to rib. He nudged aside the halter and placed damp, openmouthed kisses on one tingling breast, only inches away from her painfully tight nipple. He nuzzled into her cleavage. "I'd like to eat you up from head to toe, Mel. You taste so damn good."

This time she couldn't stop the groan. Embarrassed by her unrestrained response, she tried to add a bit of jest to the moment. "Did...did you feed me the coconut on purpose?"

He drew the tender skin of her throat against his teeth, leaving his mark behind and eliciting another raw moan. "Right now, I'd do whatever it takes. God knows we'll never have another opportunity like this one."

He didn't say it, but she knew that once they were rescued, he'd consider their time at an end. If this was all she would ever have, she didn't want to waste it.

Both his hands cupped her head, and he gently touched his mouth to hers. "Tell me you want me, too, sweetheart."

She gasped out a resounding, "Yes."

Before the agreement had finished leaving her mouth, Adam devoured it, sucking it from her, his tongue searching for and finding hers. This wasn't to be a slow interlude, evidently, given his feverish pace. But she didn't mind. She felt ready to fracture with need. With each new touch, each deeper kiss, she wanted him more.

He pulled away to shake out her skirt across the sand. Then, staring into her eyes, he shoved down his boxers. Mel swayed on her knees, he was so perfect, so sexy.

Blindly, she reached out to cup him in her palms. He made a deep sound of pleasure and pain, fisted his hands on his thighs and tilted his head back. His eyes were tightly closed.

She wrapped her fingers around his throbbing erection and stroked. When her thumb glided over the tip of him, she found a drop of moisture. Fascinated, she gently spread it around and around, until his entire body trembled.

"Enough." He gripped her wrists and pulled her away. "I can't take it, Mel. Not yet. Maybe after…"

She started to protest, but he didn't give her time. His hands cupped her breasts; his thumbs brushed her nipples. When she groaned, he said, "You're wearing too many clothes, honey. I want to see you naked. I want to kiss you everywhere."

Everywhere? It took him mere seconds to untie her halter and bare her breasts. She felt another stab of vulnerability, until he bent to greedily suck one nipple. There were no preliminaries, no forewarnings. Just the hot, moist pull of his mouth and the rough stroke of his tongue. It was so intense she tried to draw away with a short, startled exclamation. But he held her close, his callused hands spread wide on her back, gently refusing to let her retreat.

After long minutes he released her, only to switch to her other nipple.

"Adam…"

"It's the coconut, sweetheart." He nipped her with his teeth, and she trembled, tangling her fingers in the silky hair over his nape, trying to bring his mouth to hers. But he didn't budge. "I intend to drink my fill, Mel, so quit fighting me."

His fill turned out to be long minutes of sheer agony. Before he finished she was spread on her back, half on, half off the skirt, and he had settled comfortably between her thighs. She couldn't keep her hips still, thrusting up against him, but that only seemed to encourage him, to make him more ruthless. When she tugged on his hair, hurting his injured head, he captured both her wrists in one hand and pinned her arms over her head.

Leaning back on his knees, his eyes glowing in the darkness, he whispered, "It feels like a lifetime I've been waiting to see you like this." The atmosphere vibrated with his potent sexuality, making her feel decadent and drunk with erotic need.

"I can't tell you how many times I imagined coming after you, forcing you to help me get over my obsession. I wanted you just like this, open to me, accepting me."

As he spoke, he kept her arms immobile, stroking his free hand slowly down her side, closer and closer to the notch of her thighs. Tingling from the inside out, she opened herself a little wider, making it easy for him, trying to hurry him.

"That's it, Mel. Show me that you want me."

"I do."

"Not enough. Not yet."

His long fingers slid over the soft material of her shorts, right where she needed his touch most. No man had ever done this to her, and it seemed so right that

Adam would be the first to make her feel this way. She had the vague impression of knowing this was what she'd waited for. *He* was what she'd waited for.

"Please…" She felt so close to something she'd never experienced, and she desperately wanted it. She strained against him, lifting her hips as high as she could.

He pulled back. His eyes were midnight dark as he looked at her, seeing everything. With a slight shake of his head, he whispered, "Not yet, baby."

Gasping, she scrambled up and reached for him. Adam let her get as far as her knees, then caught the waistband of her shorts and started working them down. She tried to kiss him but he dodged her mouth, chuckling softly.

"It's okay, Mel. I promise. I'll take care of you."

"I want you to take care of me now."

He smiled, amused by her sudden lack of inhibition and uncharacteristic brazenness. "So impatient," he chided.

"You're the one who fed me the damn coconut!"

He slid her shorts and her panties down to her knees, then eased her onto her back to slip them the rest of the way off. He tossed them aside, and with a hand on each knee, spread her thighs wide. "Such long, sexy legs, Mel. Not at all what I imagined. Even better…" He bent to kiss the inside of one knee. "Hell, I'm glad I went overboard."

"Really?" She tried to keep her mind clear, to be coherent, but the cool brush of his silky hair on the sensitive inside of her thigh was startling. The fact that this was Adam, the town bad boy, the man who'd taken over her dreams, made it all the more incredible.

He kissed her belly a few inches below her belly button, then licked the spot. "Absolutely," he said with a throaty groan, then started licking his way downward.

"*Adam.*"

His mouth closed over her, and she stiffened at the acute pleasure. Never in her wildest imagination had she been able to aptly prepare for such a thing. Her muscles went taut while her insides seemed fluid. His rasping tongue delved and stroked and licked, and when he slipped one long finger inside her she climaxed with a raw groan that ripped from her throat and echoed around the quiet island. Adam held her there, insatiable, refusing to let the pleasure dwindle until her body went utterly limp.

He released her, gently lowering her thighs and moving to her side. She felt so drained, she didn't at first realize that he had separated himself from her. Then she felt his hand cup her breast.

"Your heart is still pounding," he said with deep satisfaction.

"That's…that's good." A heartbeat, considering she felt like she'd died, was definitely a promising sign.

She could hear his smile in the way he spoke. "You didn't do a very good job of staying on the skirt. You're more in the sand than out of it."

What was he babbling about? What difference did it make if she was in the sand? Blindly, she reached out to him, wanting to draw him close again. He caught her hand and held it. "Mel, I lied about the coconut."

He obviously thought her beyond naive, bordering on stupid. But she played along. "No aphrodisiac?"

"Of course not. But you did want me."

Very slowly, his words sank in. She heard the wonder and the insistence. She turned her head to face him. "I still do, Adam."

"Are you sure?"

He sounded uncertain, and for a man like Adam, that had to be unique. It was her turn to smile. Despite the lethargy that tried to rule her body, she rolled on top of him. He gladly went to his back and helped hold her in place, his hands firm on her bottom. She kissed his nose, his bristly chin. "No woman needs an aphrodisiac when you're around. You *breathe* and women want to jump your bones."

"You were never interested, Mel." He stroked her hair and gave her a slight smile. "No matter what I did, you managed to turn up your nose at me like I didn't exist."

Her eyes widened. "You really think that?" Then another thought invaded her fogged brain and she asked, "Do you mean to tell me you constantly provoked me just to get my attention?"

She might not have believed him, despite the recent display of his desire, if she hadn't seen the look in his eyes. But there was so much feeling there, so much raw emotion.

His hands cupped her head, his thumb brushed her cheek. "I'm sorry I was sometimes mean. As a kid, it seemed so damn unfair that you had everything, even things I hadn't dared dream of. You sort of represented everything that was missing in my life, all the stuff my parents worked so hard for but could never get."

She felt the prickle of tears and knew he wouldn't appreciate her sympathy. She swallowed hard.

"But somewhere along the way," he continued, "I started wanting you, not the material things you had. I'd stopped being mean by the time we were thirteen, Mel, but you didn't notice. You still avoided me." With a smile, he said, "You could get that pretty little nose so high in the air, I could have thrown myself at your feet and you wouldn't have seen me."

He was so wrong, but how could she explain all the various things he'd made her feel over the years? Yes, she'd often been angry at him, but she'd also felt alive whenever he was near. Adam never ignored her like the rest of the town did. He didn't give her only distant politeness. And he didn't hide what he felt behind proper manners, as her parents were wont to do. Her mother and father loved her, she'd never doubted that. But they considered an excess of emotion uncouth. They'd always been careful in how they expressed their feelings.

Not Adam. No, he teased and harassed and provoked—and she'd always responded to him, whether he knew it or not. In many ways, she'd equally dreaded and looked forward to her daily confrontations with him.

Twining her fingers in his chest hair, she said, "I was never...indifferent to you, Adam."

He gave her a crooked smile. "No, most times you hated me. And all I could think about was getting you out of your dainty little pants. Hell, there were days I'd get hard just seeing you in town or in school. You had a way of walking, like a queen, that drove me crazy. Even when I thought you were skinny—"

"I *am* skinny."

He shook his head. "No. You're thin, but you've got all the right curves in all the right places. If I'd known what you were hiding under those schoolgirl jumpers, I'd never have survived puberty."

She felt her cheeks heat, and Adam hugged her closer. His gaze was hot, probing. "I wanted you so bad, Mel, it's a wonder I survived. But I always knew you were out of bounds."

Daringly, she slipped her hand down his side to his

hip. Hard muscle and bone moved as he shifted from her touch. "I'm not out of bounds now." His eyes closed; his breathing came faster. Melanie leaned forward and kissed his chin. "Now, there's just you and me—and I want you."

He gripped her buttocks even tighter and rocked her against the long length of his erection. "I need to be inside you, sweetheart."

She wasn't experienced and couldn't tease as well as he. Already she wanted him again and felt no shame in admitting it. "Yes, please."

He laughed on a shaky breath. "You always were so damn proper."

"What we're doing now is far from proper, Adam Stone, and you know it."

His hands shifted, stroking her thighs. "All right, not proper. But you have to admit it feels damn right."

Nothing had ever felt more right in her entire life. Being with Adam seemed totally natural, because Adam was so natural. Loving him would be so easy. But nothing for the future had changed, and she doubted it ever would, not with the way Adam resented her background. But for right now, it just didn't matter.

Quickly rolling her onto her back, Adam sat up and reached for his bag. He lifted out a small foil pack and hastily tore it open with his teeth.

Melanie watched him in fascination. "Are you really such a hound dog that you carry condoms everywhere?"

Sitting by her side, he placed one hand on her belly and stroked. "Mel...I travel a lot, honey. And I avoid commitments like the plague."

Her eyes closed, both from the pain of his admission and the gentle stroking of his rough palm.

"I'm a man," he continued. His control seemed tightly leashed, but ready to break at any moment. "I enjoy sex, I won't lie about that. But as a rule, I don't believe in one-night stands."

She shifted, not really wanting details, unable to imagine him with someone else in just this way.

"Melanie, look at me."

She did, surprised by the use of her full name.

"I quit prowling after high school, sweetheart. But I am human, so I carry protection whether I plan on doing anything or not. I guess I'm old-fashioned enough to think if you make a baby, you should be a father, and I'm not ready to take a chance on that yet."

Melanie turned her face away. He couldn't have been more blunt, and while his words hurt, she understood. Adam had been given very little in life, and his attitude was actually commendable.

If only her heart weren't already involved.

"Mel?"

Choking back the hurt, she looked at him and smiled. "You talk too damn much, Stone, you know that?"

"And you're just a bit demanding." He pulled her on top of him again and situated her until she sat astride his hips. "I like it." Automatically, Melanie braced her hands on his chest and tightened her thighs. Slowly, he entered her.

She groaned at the incredible tightness.

"Mel?" His voice was strained, filled with disbelief.

"Not now, Adam." Later, when she could catch her breath, she'd explain to him why she'd waited so long to experience sex. But now the experiencing was at hand, and she didn't want to be distracted for a single moment.

Adam's chest rose and fell with his labored breaths. He pressed deeper. "Damn, you're snug." Every muscle in his arms and shoulders pulled taut with restraint.

She tipped her head back and concentrated on relaxing, on accepting him.

"Yeah. All the way, honey," he urged. "All the way…"

The natural resistance of her body gave way, and he buried himself completely inside her.

Mel dropped forward against his chest, overwhelmed with his size and strength. His fingers bit into her buttocks, holding her and his control tightly. Then he broke.

"I'm sorry," he growled through clenched teeth, even as he rolled her to her back. He thrust smoothly, deeply, lifting her hips high into the rhythm of his. Heat poured off his body.

Stunned, Melanie felt the pressure building again and she held on tight. His sudden fierceness fired her own. The friction was exquisite, the weight of his body on hers, his scent. As she started to climax, Adam pressed his face into the side of her neck and groaned out his own release.

Afterward they lay limp, both overheated, their limbs tangled. Melanie thought it was the most wondrous experience imaginable. Finally, as if the effort cost him, Adam shifted to her side, then tucked her close again. "Sleep."

She didn't need to be told twice. There in the tranquillity of the island, the moon shadows of palm leaves dancing over the white sand, the salty breeze from the ocean touching her skin, she felt more peace than she'd felt in all her life. Sleeping there with Adam was the easiest thing she'd ever done.

Loving, and leaving him, would be the hardest.

6

ADAM OPENED HIS EYES, not certain what had awakened him, and squinted against the rising sunshine. He noticed several things at once. Melanie was no longer at his side, the day was hazy, promising rain, and a huge, smelly pelican stood over him, its expression rapt, staring at his naked body.

Adam quickly scrambled back, scraping his bare butt on the fine sand. The pelican boldly scrambled after him, keeping pace. Jumping to his feet, Adam tried to intimidate the bird by making shooing motions with his arms and yelling, "Scat!" The bird lifted its enormous wings and opened its baggy beak in a silent but alarming threat.

Adam froze. Where the hell was Melanie? Watching the bird with one eye, he called, "Mel!"

She stuck her head out of the empty shack. "You're awake!"

He didn't dare look away from the pelican. "I'm being attacked, damn it."

Dividing his glances between Mel and the bird, Adam caught the way Melanie stared, perusing his body in minute detail. A lesser man might have blushed, her look was so thorough. Of course, most men wouldn't have been preoccupied defending themselves against a curious bird.

Adam watched Mel leap nimbly out of the doorway and start toward them at an angle. She wore her halter and the silky tap pants and she was the sexiest thing he'd ever seen in his entire life.

His palms began to sweat.

"I think he might want food. I tossed some coconut and strawberries to him earlier, but he wouldn't go away."

Adam inched closer to her, intending to protect her with his body if need be. "I think they only eat fish."

The pelican didn't like him moving around and fanned his wings as a warning. Adam halted. He turned slightly to Mel, but she had her gaze directed on lower parts, which caused something of an immediate reaction in his body.

"Sweetheart, there's not a damn thing I'd like more this morning than to indulge your interest, but I don't want my eyes—or more important body parts—plucked at by our feathered guest while I'm distracted by you."

"Oh." She forced her attention to the bird. "He's kind of cute, isn't he?"

"You must be kidding."

The bird took a small, mean leap at Adam and he yelped, stumbling back. Being naked, he felt even more graceless than otherwise.

"Be still, Adam. You're frightening him."

She *had* to be kidding. "Honey, find me a rock."

Appalled, Melanie turned on him and pointed a finger. "Don't you dare!" The bird, startled by her command, turned to flee. But on his way, he snatched up her underpants, resting on a pile of palm leaves, and flew away with them.

Melanie's eyes were huge. "Now look what you've done!"

"Me?" Adam did his best not to laugh. And he

couldn't very well hold a grudge against the bird. "You're the one who shouted. And for your information, I had no intention of hitting the damn bird with a rock, I just wanted to scare it away."

The bird soared down the island, out of sight. Hands on her hips, Melanie stared after it. "I washed out our stuff and left it on the leaves to dry. Now what will we do?"

"Our stuff?"

"Our...respective underthings."

Adam, having resisted her as long as he could, drew her close in the circle of his arms. "Why'd you leave me this morning?"

Mel toyed with the hair on his chest, avoiding his gaze. "I woke early so I decided to do some...stuff."

"What kind of stuff?" Already it was hard for him to carry on a conversation. She was soft and sweet and he knew her body well, knew how easily, how hotly, she responded to him. She'd combed her hair and made use of his toothpaste; he could smell the minty flavor on her breath. Her skin, sun-warmed and glowing, felt silky soft beneath his hands.

"I washed out our clothes, like I said. And I tidied up the shack in case we need to go in. The air smells rainy to me." She peeked at him, then away. "I also explored a little down the beach. A lot more of the same, except there's a mango tree there that has—"

Adam cut her off, his mood quickly changing when he thought of all the things that could have happened to her. "You took off down the beach without me?"

She looked surprised by his accusing tone. "So?"

Without even realizing it, he gripped her upper arms. "Mel, the sun's just coming up."

"There was enough light for me to see."

He wanted to shake her. "What would you have done if you'd run into another snake? Or a swarm of those damn beetles? What if you'd fallen and hit your head, or stepped on something sharp?"

She pulled away and stared at him. "I'm a big girl, Adam. I can take care of myself."

"Ha! Big girls don't go running screaming down the beach because of a little cockroach—"

"A swarm of huge cockroaches!"

"—and they aren't afraid to stick so much as a big toe in the ocean." He no sooner said it and saw her face blanch than he felt disgust for himself. Her fear of the water was real, if exaggerated, and he'd found it endearing, not something to ridicule her over. But he could tell by her quivering lip and rigid stance that he'd crossed the line.

He sighed. "Mel…"

She bit her lip to still it, and her hands fisted. After two deep breaths she very calmly, very coldly, said, "I am a coward and I freely admit it. I'm afraid of the water, or rather, things lurking in the water. But I can damn well carry my own weight here. I'm not the pampered little girl you remember. I do all the things normal women do, like go to college, work—even break engagements!"

"I didn't mean—"

That stubborn, adorable chin of hers lifted and she cut him off. "I cleaned out the shack so we can inhabit it, and yes, I did run into a few snakes. While I don't like them, I am quite capable of shooing them off with a long stick."

"Honey…"

"I also collected enough fruit for our breakfast and I

got a dozen pricks on my fingers from my efforts." She thrust her hands in front of his face, glaring.

Smiling inside, Adam took her fingers and examined the small scratches. "Blackberry bushes?"

"And some of that stupid grass. It's as sharp as needles."

"You didn't need to do all that, babe. And I'm sorry I said anything about the water."

She jerked her hands away in renewed pique. "The point is, if I choose to go exploring, I will. I don't need your permission or your protection." Then she sneered, "Or are you going to lie some more about wild boars?"

"You read my *Key to the Keys*?"

She thumped him on the chest with one small fist. "I'm not an idiot, damn it! I don't need to read your dumb guidebook to know there aren't any wild boars here."

She was so adorable in her anger, and he was naked and hard. It was difficult to take part in the conversation when all he really wanted to do was lay her down and slide into her body again. Last night he'd tried to make her see how different she was from any other woman he'd been with. Sheer physical gratification couldn't compare with the deep, primal possessiveness he felt with her. But he knew by the look on her face she hadn't understood. She thought she was just one more woman in a long line of conquests. And this morning, being in a saner frame of mind, he wasn't about to tell her no other woman had mattered, not when he always pretended they were her. That was a little too heavy to lay on a woman after only one night.

"Mel, I don't want you wandering off alone because it isn't safe, boar or no boar. I have no idea what kinds of snakes are on the island, if they're poisonous or not. The shack looks ready to collapse, so until we can decide if it's safe enough to be in, I don't want either of us wandering off alone. Okay?"

His cajoling tone and apologetic expression must have gotten to her. "You're expressing yourself much better this time around, Stone."

He grinned. She obviously didn't know how badly it scared him to think of her getting hurt. "I'm naked, horny as hell, and you're running around in this sexy little outfit, looking good enough to be breakfast. How do you expect me to act?"

Her mouth opened and closed twice, then she looked down and started toying with his chest hair again. He liked her like this, all sweet and innocent and shy. His hands slid over her hips, appreciating the feel of her firm softness beneath the slippery material.

"I looked at you this morning."

Adam froze while kissing her neck. "Is that right?"

She nodded, bumping his chin. "You're very...sexy, too."

Grinning from ear to ear, he put one finger beneath her chin and lifted her face so he could see her eyes. "Am I hearing this right? You took advantage of my exhaustion to sate your curiosity on my poor body?"

A blush exploded on her cheeks and her long lashes drifted down to hide her expression, but she smiled. "Yes. And I enjoyed myself, too. You...affect me, Adam. Once I woke up and saw you, it was impossible to go back to sleep. I had to find something to do so I wouldn't attack you, but I knew you needed your rest after hurting your head."

"My head is fine, feeling better by the second." He kissed her long and deep, his tongue tasting her, enticing her. "You should have wakened me," he growled between nibbling on her lips.

"You're awake now."

"And you're overdressed." One small tug, and her halter dropped to her waist.

This time was no less frantic than the night before, and afterward, as they both lay sated and hot and damp from their exertions and the rising humidity, Adam frowned. He couldn't quite reconcile the way she made him feel, complete but still hungry, at peace but still turbulent. He'd always known there was something there, an irresistible chemistry that drew him in, but he'd thought it all one-sided. Now, seeing her naked beside him, panting for breath, her scream of pleasure at the time of her climax still ringing in his ears, he realized how wrong he'd been. She'd moved with him, kept pace with him, every step of the way.

Yet she'd been a virgin.

Laying a hand on her damp belly, relishing the fact that she still trembled, he said, "Tell me about yourself, Mel. What you've been up to."

She cocked one pale blue eye open to peer at him, and groaned. "I think you've killed me."

He laughed. "With pleasure." Leaning down to kiss her, he added, "You're one demanding little lady."

"You'd make me blush if I had the strength."

"You want me to show you exactly how much strength you still have?" He drifted his fingers down her belly.

Melanie caught his wrist and moaned. "No, I'll talk."

"Good. Start with this idiot fiancé of yours."

"He's not my fiancé, not anymore, and he's also not an idiot. In fact, he's very intelligent, successful—

pretty special, really." She sighed, then tilted her head to the side to smile at him. "Jerry Marshall is actually considered quite a catch. He's not as tall as you, but he's handsome. Hair as black as my own, great teeth."

Adam made a sound of disgust. "I don't give a damn about his teeth. Why the hell haven't you slept with him?"

There was that seductive blush again, making his muscles twitch and his heart pound. When would her potent effect on him diminish? Never? He couldn't accept that prospect and determinedly pushed the problem from his mind. They were still eons apart, and he had a hell of a lot yet to accomplish before he could even begin to think of settling down, especially with a woman like Melanie Tucker.

But she'd given him her virginity. In too many ways to count, he felt she was his already.

"I don't know, Adam. The time just never seemed right." She wouldn't look at him, choosing to stare at the sky. "Jerry's practice kept him pretty busy, and our time together was usually spent at social gatherings or working. I guess I wasn't overly anxious to get intimate, and Jerry seemed content to wait."

"What an ass."

She smiled. "Well, I'd expect that attitude from a hound dog like you."

"I told you last night, I'm not nearly as insatiable as you want to think I am."

Her eyes widened and she leaned up far enough to look at their naked bodies. "Could have fooled me."

"It's different with you." He kissed her nose and spoke in a whisper. "You make me crazy." Maybe he was a hound dog, after all, because he sure as hell couldn't look at her, couldn't even think of her, without wanting her in the most elemental ways possible. "How long have you been broken up with this guy?"

"About a month." She cuddled closer and rested her head on his chest. "I wanted to get a different job, something more challenging. He didn't want me to. My parents agreed with him."

"What kind of job did you want?"

She tipped her head to look at him. "I don't know. Something fun, exciting. Working for Jerry was...well, it was boring."

"Maybe that's because Jerry was boring."

"Most women don't think so." She smiled slightly, then admitted, "I made a lot of money on the stock market, and by investing in real estate. I wanted to get more involved with that. I seem to have a knack for it."

"Real estate?" That was one of his big interests.

"Yes." She leaned on one elbow. "Adam, my money is all my own, separate from my parents."

That surprised him. Somehow he'd always figured she'd simply live off an inheritance, like every other pampered rich kid. "So you've made your own fortune?"

She nodded. "I have a way with numbers, and with property. Some day I'll inherit my parents' money, but for now, I don't want it or need it."

Ridiculously, he felt proud of her. She was more independent than he'd thought, and it pleased him. "Why not take what's coming to you? You get along with your folks, don't you?"

"Yes. I just like it better when I'm not answerable to anyone but myself." She turned her face toward him, and her smoky eyes nearly did him in. That is, until she spoke. "I want to buy your resort, Adam."

Her words felt like a punch to the chest, making him

clench his teeth. After his mother had been forced to accept charity from the town to bury his father, he swore it would never happen again. Taking refuge from his painful memories, he moved on top of Melanie and parted her thighs.

She clung to him, accepting him. "Adam, please just let me explain what I—"

"Be quiet, Mel." He gently, inexorably pushed himself into her, his groan mingling with hers, their gazes locked.

Melanie waited until he was completely buried inside her, then whispered, "Adam, I've made up my mind. I'm buying the resort. From what you've said, it's a good deal, so—"

"Damn it." He began to thrust, and she held on tight, her fingertips digging deep into his shoulders. He wanted to drown out her words, the fact that she could do what he couldn't, that she had enough money and he still didn't. It proved her right; nothing and neither of them had really changed, after all. They were each older and wiser, but their placement in the world was the same; they were still at opposite ends of the scale.

All his life, he'd fought hard against a society that said if you were born with money, life was easy, but if you had to earn it, there was a whole new set of rules. He'd learned early on what the main rule was: those with money did as they pleased. Melanie included. She really didn't care what he wanted, she was just appeasing her ridiculous guilt.

Right now what he wanted most was for Melanie to give in to him, to be female to his male. At least in this he had the upper hand.

She quickened beneath him, and her teeth bit into the muscle on his shoulder. He flinched, and at the same time his touted control broke. He was a wild man—primal, complete.

Afterward, he didn't wait for his breathing to calm, for his heartbeat to slow. He came jerkily to his feet and stood looking down at her. So damn beautiful. So damn rich. Tears shone on her long black lashes, making her blue eyes liquid and bright. Her breasts shimmered with her gasping, ragged breaths.

He walked away, straight into the ocean until he stood waist deep. The water was cool, and with clouds covering the sun, he should have felt comfortable. Instead, he was stricken by the flash heat of anger and despair. He wanted to rail against the world. He hadn't used a condom that last time. And he wouldn't touch her again.

He thought of her, not more than two yards away, looking earthy, warm, satisfied, everything a woman—his woman—should be. He ground his teeth and reminded himself it wouldn't be for long. Surely they'd be missed soon and then someone would come for them. Someone had to rescue him, before he lost *everything*—his head, his heart, and his self-respect.

"SHE'S SUCH A damn tease," Adam accused.

Silence and a bold stare were the only reply from his feathered companion.

"Just look at her. She knows damn good and well I'm trying to be noble, trying to leave her alone, so what does she do? She starts flaunting, that's what!"

The bird waddled closer, as if enthralled by what Adam had to say. Adam shook his head. Leave it to Mel to befriend a big ugly bird. A bird who had stolen her panties.

She'd begun bribing the pelican two days ago, the

same morning he'd sworn not to touch her again, by offering up a few colorful shells she'd found in the cove. Aladdin, named after the king of thieves, had swiped the shells and flown off, then returned later that day to steal again. He'd taken Adam's makeshift bandage when he'd pulled it off to dunk his head in the ocean, trying to cool down from the heat Mel generated, and the frustration of resisting her. He'd also stolen Adam's tie—and anything else he could get hold of.

Adam never complained to Melanie when she laughed at Aladdin's antics. He couldn't trust himself to talk to her much at all since deciding to leave her alone. Sleeping next to her for two nights without making love to her was the hardest thing he'd ever done.

He still held her; he'd done his best to comfort her and make her feel safe. Not that it had been necessary. She'd adapted better than he'd ever thought possible. Not once did she complain about the heat, or the lack of privacy, or sleeping in the open either on the sandy beach, or when it rained, in the ramshackle shack. She looked more enticing than ever with the touch of sun on her cheeks, and she never hesitated to give him hell when she thought he deserved it, which was most of the time. He admired her spunk and her capability.

He told himself it wouldn't be fair to make love to her now that he knew how innocent she was. She'd obviously been waiting for that one special man, and in spite of all the ways he'd improved his life, he was still leagues away from being Mr. Right.

Making love to her wouldn't be fair to him, either. Hell, given half a chance, he'd fall in love with her all over again, and then where would he be?

She had her heart set on buying the resort, on giving

him back what he'd lost. She didn't doubt that she would succeed, which only proved again the differences between them. Mel knew her money would buy her whatever she wanted. It always had.

The pelican shuffled closer, keeping a watchful eye on Adam, who was keeping a watchful eye on Melanie. The rain, coming down in a fresh, warm shower, insulated them in the quiet eroticism of the island. Palms swayed under the gentle wind, the ocean looked agitated with its rippling surface, and Melanie, God love her free-spirited nature, revelled in it all. Little by little, she'd blossomed on the island, giving in to its erotic lure.

She'd taken his soap and shampoo and dashed into the rain, then proceeded to bathe, slowly, unselfconscious, fully aware that he sat in the doorway of the shack utterly spellbound. The first time she'd retreated down the beach to wash, but now she seemed determined to drive him insane. And she succeeded admirably.

Mel could sit on a rock to watch the sunset and he'd go crazy with lust. His need was so powerful, he hurt, but Adam wouldn't have looked away from her for all the resorts in Florida.

"Aw, hell," he blurted, making Aladdin jump warily, "Who am I fooling? I love her already. I never stopped loving her. Doubt I ever will. I'm fighting a losing battle here and I know it."

The pelican gave him a vague look of sympathy, then opened his wings wide...and snatched a sock from Adam's bag before soaring away.

Outraged, Adam stood and shook his fist at the bird. "I'm going to find a rock yet, you feathered bag of bones!"

On the beach, Melanie crossed her arms over her middle and laughed out loud. Her midnight hair hung in sodden ringlets around her face. And her body...damn, she'd finally slipped off her clothes. The bird was instantly forgotten. Nobility couldn't be expected to stand up to such provocation, could it?

With renewed purpose, Adam leapt off the stoop and headed in her direction. His fate was sealed, but fate had allotted him this special time with Melanie, and from now on he'd take advantage of every moment.

Melanie, aptly reading his intent, squealed and turned to run. Her long legs ate up the distance across the wet sand. The view from behind her was the stuff dreams were made of, so Adam let her stay two yards ahead of him.

Darting behind a squat palm tree, she playfully yelled, "What do you want, Stone?"

He paused several feet away, enjoying her antics. Anticipation would only make the conquest that much sweeter. After two days of deprivation, his body vibrated with lust, and the look he sent her was hot with need. "Come here, sweetheart."

"What's that?" she called, her eyes lit with laughter. "You want me to fix us some lunch?"

She could be such an imp. He'd never imagined this playful side to her. She'd always been so shy, so withdrawn. Of course, he'd never imagined she'd thrive so well on the bare existence of a deserted island, either.

Or that she'd willingly accept him as a lover.

He shook his head, watching her closely. "Yeah, I'm hungry, all right." Hooking his hands in his shorts, he began shoving the wet material down his hips.

She peeked around the tree at him and yelped. "Shall...shall I fix another fruit salad?"

Rain dribbled down her belly, caught in her feminine curls, then trailed down her thighs. He swallowed hard. "You can fix yourself right here." He pointed to the sand in front of him. "I'll take it from there."

"No strawberries? No coconut?"

As she spoke, she tried to inch away from the tree, preparing to run. Adam leapt out and caught her, hauling her close to his naked chest. With a startled squeal, she almost slipped away, then laughed hilariously when Adam hooked his leg behind hers and they both fell to the ground. Rain ran from his shoulders to her breasts. He stared hungrily at one stiff nipple. "I'm sick to death of fruit," he muttered, then drew her deep into the heat of his mouth.

Mel's fingers gripped his head, and she tugged until he lifted it enough to look at her. "I thought... I thought maybe you were sick of me."

"No!" He could see the confusion in her eyes, the vulnerability. He hadn't meant to hurt her. "I could never get my fill of you, Mel. I want you too much." He touched her mouth with his fingertips, then gruffly admitted, "Sometimes, when things were rough, dreaming of you like this was the only thing that got me through."

Even in the pouring rain, he could see her eyes fill with tears. "You don't want all of me."

They were both drenched, their skin slick. He moved silkily against her. "Yeah, I do. Every damn inch of you."

"No." He started to pull back, but her fingers gripped his hair and held him close. She gave him a swift, hard kiss. "You want my body, Adam, but not me, not who I am."

"You're not making any sense, Mel." But he was afraid he understood completely.

"You don't want my money. No, just listen!" She wrapped her slender thighs around his waist, holding him securely. "You resent who and what I am. If I even mention my money, you clam up and refuse to share yourself."

"Because I don't need your damn money!"

"Why?" she asked quietly. "Because it's mine? If I was a bank offering a low-interest loan, you wouldn't hesitate, would you? But my money is somehow considered tainted."

"Damn it, Melanie…"

"You're hanging onto the differences in our backgrounds, even though we've both changed."

"Don't you see, honey? Nothing's changed, not really. If we hadn't landed on this damn island, you'd never have given me the time of day."

"Adam." She said his name like a chastisement. "I know your life wasn't easy, but *I* didn't make it hard. In many ways, mine was difficult, too."

"Because of me."

"It doesn't matter now. If it wasn't for you, I would have drowned. Even if I'd made it to shore on my own, which is doubtful, the thought of being here alone terrifies me. But you've made it seem like an adventure. That's the way you are, Adam. You've been working all your life to save your mother and Kyle, and you *did* save me. You can deny it all you like, but you're still a hero. My hero. You saved me, and I owe you."

He hardened his heart against the plea in her eyes. When they got off the island and she was once again surrounded by her family and elite friends, she'd come to her senses. More likely than not, she'd be embarrassed over their shared intimacy, over her lack of inhibition with him.

Just thinking about it made his blood burn, and he stared at her. "All right, so I saved you. But you can forget the resort. I already consider myself fully and adequately paid." To emphasize his meaning, he thrust himself against her—and watched her expression crumble.

Adam rolled to his side, letting the rain lash his face and cool his shame while Melanie scrambled to her feet.

He heard her panting breaths over the downpour, could feel her tension. Her words were choked with tears when she shouted, "You're a mean, miserable bastard, Adam Stone!"

Adam flinched, but otherwise didn't move. What could he say? That she was right? There would be no explanations, no words to appease her. How could he explain what he didn't understand himself? He only knew he couldn't let himself get drawn in, because eventually, she'd realize the truth—that he was just a man, still working to get ahead and often failing.

He scrubbed at his face and silently accepted that the dream had ended.

Two seconds later Melanie let out a small screech and snatched up her shorts and halter. She darted behind a mangrove tree and frantically began to dress.

Alarmed, Adam jumped to his feet, expecting to see the wild boar he'd relentlessly teased her about.

What he saw instead was almost worse: a small fishing boat headed their way. At the helm, a hard-looking man who seemed impervious to the rain, stared to-

ward them in disbelief. Though he was too far out to
see them clearly, possessive rage washed through
Adam. If the boat had shown up minutes earlier, its
captain might have seen Mel naked.

The boat slowed and began idling toward the beach.
Adam pulled on his sand-covered shorts and walked
into the ocean to meet their rescuer.

7

"SO YOU HAVEN'T spoken to her since this Flynn Ryder guy showed up, right?"

Adam gave a sigh of disgust as he and his younger brother, Kyle, rounded the corner of a heavily flowered courtyard and headed around the quaint building to the beach behind it. Tourists abounded at the newly opened resort, making Adam's temper burn. The resort should have been his. But the little witch had bought it back. For him.

Damn her.

He'd gone over the whole story a dozen times, but Kyle still hadn't run out of questions. "There was nothing to say after that. We both felt damn foolish for getting stranded in the first place. The shoaling around the island makes it dangerous for boats to get too close, so people don't visit it often. If it hadn't been for Flynn, who knows how long we might have been there? The idiots that lost us didn't even know we were missing, so nothing had been reported."

"Eventually I'd have figured things out and sent the cavalry," Kyle assured him. "But you never did say what Flynn was doing there."

No, he hadn't. Flynn Ryder evidently owned his own resort on a neighboring island, but it was Aladdin leaving a trail of clothing around the area—specifically Melanie's panties—that had caused Flynn to investigate the smaller island. The minute Adam had explained they were both from Ohio, Flynn had nodded understanding and taken them to civilization.

Adam had felt like a complete fool over the whole thing, especially when Melanie told Flynn that Adam had saved her. Flynn had given him a skeptical look but hadn't bothered to comment. In fact, he'd said very little to Adam. But he'd talked up a storm with Melanie. Not that he had much choice. Melanie, deliberately provoking Adam, he was sure, had asked Flynn dozens of questions on the daily operations of owning a resort. Adam had considered throwing her overboard again. In the end, he'd simply ignored her.

Adam and Kyle stopped in a crowd of bikini-clad guests and looked around for a familiar dark head. The desk clerk had claimed she was out here—waiting.

"You're leaving something out, Adam."

Damn, sometimes his brother was too astute. Hedging, he asked, "Why do you think so?"

Kyle tapped the papers Adam clutched in one fist. "She bought you a resort. You're pissed off about it. She insisted on seeing you in person, and you're giving in. It doesn't take a genius to figure it out."

"Does it take a genius to figure out it's none of your business?"

"Why did you drag me along, then?"

Because he hadn't wanted to tempt fate by seeing her alone again. He felt terrible for the things he'd said, the way he'd treated her that last day. Once they'd reached a hotel and been given separate rooms, Adam had tried to contact her, to apologize and do the old see-ya-later routine. He hadn't wanted to part with hurt feelings, not when she meant so much to him. And he'd wanted her to know how to reach him, just in case his forgetfulness with the condom became an issue. But she'd already checked out. And he'd been feeling sick ever since.

Then a week ago he'd gotten her damn letter saying she'd bought the resort back for him, just as she'd promised to do. She had to have paid considerably more than he would have, just to get the new owner to sell. And looking around, he could easily see all the extra money she'd invested already. In just over a month she'd made the place look stunning, much as he'd always envisioned it.

She'd done it all, and put his damn name on the deed.

The papers crumpled in his fist when he finally spotted her sitting at an outdoor bar situated ideally beneath a cluster of ripe palms. Her shapely bottom was perched on a bar stool, her long legs and smooth shoulders mostly bare. The dress she wore was tiny, snug, and matched the floral decor of the many patio tables and open umbrellas.

Where the hell had she gotten that getup? And since when did she flaunt herself for the masses, rather than for his private pleasure?

Kyle evidently followed his gaze, for he let loose with a long, low, admiring whistle. "Holy cow. That's Melanie Tucker, isn't it?"

Adam snapped his head around to stare at his brother. "You remember her?"

"I was only a couple grades behind her in school. And being the richest kid in town, she really stood out."

Adam thought it was more her eyes that made her noticeable, and when he looked at her, he saw those eyes staring directly at him. Slowly, she slid off the stool and started in his direction. She was barefoot, lightly tanned, her blue eyes looking bluer than ever.

His heart lodged in his throat, and he had to swallow hard twice to regain his composure. Every muscle in his body twitched, and he struggled to relax. Which did nothing about the erection making his appreciation of her rather apparent. In his worn jeans, there was no way to hide it. He'd missed her so damn much.

"Adam." She stopped just a few inches from him and simply stood there, waiting.

Kyle stepped forward and extended his hand. "Miss Tucker. Nice to see you again."

She drew her gaze from Adam with an effort. "You're Kyle, Adam's younger brother, right?"

Adam listened with half an ear as the introductions commenced. She looked so good, and he'd been sick with missing her ever since he'd realized she was gone forever. Then he'd gotten the damn letter....

He came back to his senses in a flash and thrust the deed toward her. "I don't want this."

She smiled, lifting her chin high. "Tough. It's yours."

"Then I'll sell it and mail you back your check."

"You can't. We're co-owners. You might not have noticed or read all the small print given your...rather quick temper, but we have equal control of the resort."

"That's impossible."

"No, it's a fact. I told you, I have a knack for real estate, so I know what I'm doing. Everything's perfectly legal. And you were right, this place is wonderful. Much too good to pass up."

Kyle laughed, earning a glare from Adam. "Now, Adam, come on. I still don't understand why you're being so pigheaded about this."

Adam turned on his brother, deciding he was a safer target than Mel. He didn't have to fight the urge to kiss his brother. Through clenched teeth, he muttered, "We make our own way now, Kyle."

"No, *you* make our way. I haven't had a hell of a lot to do with it."

Adam drew back a step, scowling fiercely. "That's ridiculous. I'm your brother. Besides, you've been going to college."

Kyle turned to smile at Melanie. "Did you know he mostly paid my way through college? With what I made working part-time, it would have taken me years to pay back student loans. He also bought my mother a house. That's part of the reason he had to do some fancy financing to get the money together for this resort. If he didn't feel so responsible for us, he'd be rolling in dough."

"Kyle…"

Adam's warning went unheeded. "We're damn proud of him and all he's done. Even before Dad died, Adam's always been my hero."

There was that word again, making him edgy. He scowled at Kyle. "We're family. You've done plenty for me, too."

Kyle clapped Adam on the back. "He's always been one hell of a big brother. I was really looking forward to settling down here, soaking up some sun, using my degree in business to help get things going. But if he won't accept it…"

Mel's smile turned gentle and sweet. "I didn't know all that about Adam. But it doesn't surprise me. I think of him as a hero, too. After he rescued me from drowning, I knew he could do anything he set his mind to— which is why I didn't want him to miss this opportunity just because he likes to wallow in stubborn, misplaced pride."

Adam felt smothered in their collective praise. "For the last damn time, Mel, I *fell* in. I did not jump in after you!"

Very quietly, and with supreme confidence, she whispered, "But you would have."

How the hell was he supposed to argue with that? It was the truth, and he could see there was no point in denying it. They stared at each other, both oblivious to the tourists milling around them. Kyle cleared his throat and said, "I think I'll just go look around a little."

Adam hadn't wanted to be left alone with Mel. Not that standing on a crowded beach was alone, but he felt totally apart from the others, as if only the two of them existed. He touched her cheek. "I'm sorry, babe. I know you mean well, but I can't accept."

"You gave me so much, Adam."

He smiled. "What? I let you use my shampoo and shared my toothbrush. It's hardly the same as a costly resort."

Melanie shook her head, and sunlight glinted off her dark hair. "No, don't you understand? You gave me your strength and self-confidence. All my life I've been sheltered and pampered, and men treated me like a glass doll. But you...you treat me like a woman." She nervously licked her lips. "You make me feel sexy."

"Aw, babe..."

"I might have shared my money, Adam, but that money hadn't made me happy. Knowing you wanted me, making love with you, even arguing with you, makes me happier than I thought possible. The best time I've ever had was being stranded with you."

"Honey, you were always sexy. Almost too much so."

She treated him to a crooked grin. "Since I walked out here this morning to wait for you, I've been hit on a dozen times."

Adam scowled, his gaze scanning the crowds. "Who hit on you?"

"It's not important. My point is—"

"The point is that you need more clothes on!"

"Adam, I'm covered far more than the women in their bathing suits. And besides, I like the way you looked at me when you saw me in this outfit."

Adam stepped closer and gave in to the urge to hold her, bringing her against his chest. "It's not the outfit, Mel, it's you. Even when you wore school girl jumpers and penny loafers back in high school, you made me hard."

She blushed, but she also smiled. "You see? That's the most precious compliment I've ever gotten."

Adam rolled his eyes. "Your fiancé was an idiot."

"No." She licked her lips, and the vulnerability that sometimes clouded her eyes bit into his soul. "He wasn't an idiot, Adam. He just wasn't you.

It felt like she'd ripped his heart out. "Mel."

"And he didn't...love me."

The question was there in her beautiful blue eyes. Adam knew he owed it to her to tell her. What difference did her money make if he'd be miserable without her? In fact, he'd never felt so damn poor, so lacking in true wealth as he did when she'd left him without saying goodbye. He'd been an unhappy bastard ever since.

Before he could say anything, Kyle showed up, and he was grinning from ear to ear. "Adam, the place is perfect. Almost everything we would have done, she's taken care of. But there's still some things—"

Melanie spoke quickly. "—that could be improved on, only I've used up my savings. I need a partner to help me finish fixing things up." She drew a deep breath and clutched her hands together in front of her. "I know about buying property and what a good investment is. But I don't know much beyond that. I've got faith in this place, and I've done some cosmetic work, but there's still so much that has to be done. I can't...don't want to do it alone. So if you truly don't want to be partners with me, I'll sell you my shares of the resort. You can reimburse me over a period of time. I'll even make the interest rates fair, but I'd much rather—"

Very softly, Adam said, "I'd much rather marry you."

She let out her breath in a whoosh. "Marry me?"

Kyle grinned. "I knew it! She's the one you've always talked about. I could tell the minute you looked at her."

Adam nodded slowly, his gaze still locked with Melanie's. Melanie looked uncertain.

"Mom would harass him," Kyle explained, "about settling down, about giving her grandkids, but Adam always said he couldn't because he'd already met the most incredible woman, an icon that other women couldn't possibly measure up to."

"He said that...about me?"

Adam just smiled, watching his brother work. Kyle was smooth, much more so than Adam ever hoped to be. He could charm the socks off anyone, and though their mother didn't realize it, he was the real hound dog in the family. But Kyle was subtle, so the ladies usually didn't realize it until it was too late.

"Yeah. Adam always said you were an aristocrat and a little stuck up—"

"Hey!" Adam considered throwing his brother out to sea.

"But he made it sound real sexy." Kyle's eyes were bright with laughter.

"He did, huh?" Melanie looked unconvinced but open to suggestion.

"You betcha. So what do you think? You going to marry him so we can get this business settled?"

Melanie stared at Adam's chest. "Do you love me, Adam?"

He cupped her chin and tilted her face up. "Since I've been old enough to know what love is, you've been the one for me."

Tears welled in her eyes. "Me, too, though I didn't realize it. I just knew I watched for you and felt alive around you and that—"

"What?"

Mindful of Kyle's rapt attention, she tiptoed to whisper in his ear. "That I wanted you." She kissed his throat and wrapped her arms around him. "I knew I couldn't marry anyone else, not when all I could think of was you."

Adam dropped the deed so he could fill his hands with her. "I love you, Mel. I always have." He kissed her and vaguely heard the stirring of interest from the crowds watching them. His brother made the announcement that they were newly engaged, which earned a round of applause.

It was difficult, but Adam finally managed to pull

his mouth away from hers. "Are there empty rooms inside?"

"Too many to count. I expect we need to work on that."

"I know one room we can fill right now."

She smiled at his deep, suggestive tone, and her cheeks turned pink. "I have one reserved just for us."

Adam felt like shouting, he was so happy. "So you'll marry me and put up with Kyle and welcome my mother?"

She grinned, trying for a look of indecision when her expressive eyes already showed how happy she felt. "Well, I suppose so, as long as you know my parents are rather curious about you, too. They'll want a big wedding, but they love me, so it shouldn't be too bad."

"I won't take money from them, sweetheart," he felt compelled to warn her.

She merely shrugged. "I told you I make my own money, and they've already accepted that, even if they're not happy about it. But you can plan on them pampering our babies. I figure with your strength of will, you'll be able to keep things balanced."

Adam nearly swallowed his tongue. "Are you...?"

"Not yet." She lifted her nose into the air. "But I want to be. And soon."

"I just love a bossy woman." Without warning he scooped her into his arms and swung her in a circle. Kyle laughed when he said, "You heard the lady. I have work to do."

Kyle picked up the deed and shoved it into his pocket. "So we're keeping the place?" he shouted after his brother.

"Hell, yes." Adam grinned at Melanie. "I'm the richest man in the world. I can do anything."

SLOW BURN
Elda Minger

"Sex fascinates everyone. Anyone who denies this, in my opinion, is either lying or dead."

So says bestselling author and RITA nominee Elda Minger. Elda is well-known in the world of romance for red-hot, passionate reads that portray the ultra-sensual relationships between sassy women and incredibly sexy men. "Writing for Temptation Blaze allows me to go beyond what's been done and reach that sizzling, cutting edge."

Elda knows what she's talking about, having lectured on the subject of sex and sensuality at several universities, including UCLA, and at national writer's conferences. A native Californian, she and her family still call the Golden State home. When she is not writing, Elda enjoys reading ("That's what got me into this business in the first place!"), movies, traveling, her numerous pets, gardening and restoring the home that has been in her family for generations.

"I *love* hearing from readers. Do you enjoy reading about romantic characters as much as I enjoy writing about them?" Elda can be reached c/o Harlequin Enterprises Ltd., 225 Duncan Mill Road, Don Mills, Ontario, Canada M3B 3K9.

Prologue

FLYNN RYDER strolled along the shoreline of his private island in the Florida Keys, enjoying the tropical breeze whisper over his nearly naked body. Clad only in a worn pair of cut-off jeans, he walked barefoot in the coarse sand as he wondered if what he planned to do to his ex-wife was right.

It wasn't as if he questioned his motives often. Life had been a great teacher, and he knew most of the time he had had to act quickly, think swiftly, just to survive. But this time he'd deliberately set something in motion with the intent of bringing his wife—he never really thought of the two of them as divorced—back home to his kingdom, his corner of the world.

She would be arriving today, with no idea that he was here. With no idea that he'd engineered the entire thing. With no idea that what he wanted, more than anything in the world, more than all the money and property he'd accumulated over the last eight years, was to look into her eyes and ask her for the truth.

Flynn had to know. It ate at him, this past of his. This past he shared with Alison. Something about their separation and subsequent divorce had never felt right to him. But what wisdom had either of them had in their twenties? They'd both been possessed, in a frenzy of love, a hormonal passion that hadn't responded to wisdom and communication, but had flashed past that to hatred, blaming and finally their separation and divorce.

He'd tried to forget her. He'd tried in every way possible. But still, whenever he saw a certain shade of hair, heard a laugh that sounded the least bit like hers, glimpsed a face that even vaguely resembled Ally's, smelled that same light floral perfume—

Enough.

Flynn came to a stop and gazed over the shimmering ocean. He reached down and ruffled the ears of the black dog that stood beside him at the water's edge, patiently waiting with him for the sun to rise. Stars still sprinkled the sky as it steadily grew lighter. Sluggish waves slid up the coarse sand, then whispered back, leaving gleaming wetness in their wake. Teddy, his Lab mix and dear friend, licked his outstretched fingers and whined.

Even his dog knew.

Flynn was nervous, excited, apprehensive—a total mix of emotions he couldn't afford to give in to right now. He had to remain cool, had to remain very calm, as calm and focused and centered as he'd been when he'd sailed the ocean looking for treasure. One wrong decision when he dealt with either the ocean or a woman, and a man could find himself drowning, dying, washing up on the shore with every bone in his body broken.

With his heart broken, which as any man with any sense knew was far worse a break than a mere bone.

His heart had been broken, but he'd survived. Survived and prospered. Traveled so many miles, over land and sea. Sailed with some very fine men and found treasure far beyond his wildest imaginings. Wealth beyond compare. He'd gone on to build a resort that catered to any sensual need a person could conjure up.

PLAY...

"ROLL A DOUBLE!"

PEEL OFF LABEL AND PLACE INSIDE

GET 2 BOOKS
AND A
FABULOUS MYSTERY BONUS GIFT

ABSOLUTELY FREE!

SEE INSIDE...

(H-T-07/99)

NO RISK, NO OBLIGATION TO BUY...NOW OR EVER!

GUARANTEED

PLAY "ROLL A DOUBLE" AND YOU GET FREE GIFTS! HERE'S HOW TO PLAY:

1. Peel off label from front cover. Place it in space provided at right. With a coin, carefully scratch off the silver dice. Then check the claim chart to see what we have for you – TWO FREE BOOKS and a mystery gift – ALL YOURS! ALL FREE!

2. Send back this card and you'll receive brand-new Harlequin Temptation® novels. These books have a cover price of $3.75 each in the U.S. and $4.25 each in Canada, but they are yours to keep absolutely free.

3. There's no catch. You're under no obligation to buy anything. We charge nothing – ZERO – for your first shipment. And you don't have to make any minimum number of purchases – not even one!

4. The fact is, thousands of readers enjoy receiving books by mail from the Harlequin Reader Service®. They like the convenience of home delivery...they like getting the best new novels BEFORE they're available in stores...and they love our discount prices!

5. We hope that after receiving your free books you'll want to remain a subscriber. But the choice is yours – to continue or cancel any time at all! So why not take us up on our invitation, with no risk of any kind. You'll be glad you did!

Yet he still wasn't happy. He wasn't happy because Ally wasn't in his life. How one woman could so completely hold his heart in her hand, wrap his entire being around her little finger, both astonished and humbled him. And frightened him. He could face a storm at sea; he could dive to the depths and risk sharks, barracudas and any of the other myriad dangers that might befall him below that shimmering surface.

Yet he hadn't been able to win the heart of the only woman he'd ever loved.

That would be settled soon. Today. He would see her today, shortly after she arrived at his island and checked into his resort. He would let her believe she was safe, that she had ten glorious days of vacation ahead of her, before he announced his intentions.

He stroked Teddy's head softly as he gazed at the sky, as the sun finally peeped above the Atlantic and began to wash the horizon with pale pastel blues and mauves.

She has to still feel the way I do....

It took him a moment to realize he was whispering the words, sending them out into the morning sky like a prayer, a passionate request to the fates. He'd prayed before, in the midst of storms, when huge waves had crashed over the decks of the *Nemo*. When he and the men he'd sailed with hadn't thought they had a chance of staying alive, when thoughts of bars of gold and shimmering doubloons vanished from their minds and all they'd concentrated on was keeping a cool head and not being consumed by the fury of the storm.

Flynn closed his eyes and felt the gentle tropical trade winds on his face as he took a few deep breaths of the cool, ocean-scented air. His instincts, his intuition had been honed razorsharp by his time at sea. And he knew, without a doubt, that a different kind of storm flickered on the horizon. It wouldn't be long before everything changed.

It wouldn't be long before he saw Ally again.

1

ALISON HENNESSY peered out the window of the helicopter, barely able to contain her excitement. Below, the myriad shades of blue and green ocean made her realize how far she was from the life she normally lived. What woman in the world wouldn't have jumped at the chance of a ten-day vacation in Paradise, or rather, *at* Paradise, a world-renowned resort?

Decadent. Luxurious. Sensual. Scandalous. The words that flitted through her mind made up the public's assessment of the resort. A place for movie stars and supermodels, rock stars and royalty, Paradise didn't normally cater to the wishes of a divorced thirty-year-old landscape designer from Evanston, Illinois. But having won the stay in a national contest, Alison didn't care if she wasn't the usual sort of guest. She was going to make the most of the next ten days. She was going to hide away, let herself be pampered and indulged and do some soul searching.

Alison was going to find out what she wanted to do with the rest of her life.

She knew something was wrong. She'd felt dead inside for a long time, that horrible feeling when you knew you were just walking through your days, making it from sunrise to sunset but not really living. Alison knew her life was off track, that she just wasn't doing what made her happy to get up in the morning.

Oh, she got up in the morning. And she loved her

work, loved creating gardens and areas of great beauty with various plants, with colorful flowers, with herbs and ornamental shrubs. She'd started her landscaping business with her college roommate almost six years ago, and she and Kate had built it into a flourishing enterprise. So flourishing that weeks went by where she did nothing but work very long hours that completely took over her life.

But something was missing.

Flynn.

She pushed the thought determinedly out of her mind and concentrated on the water below. She could see an island approaching and clasped her hands tightly together.

Paradise. Both the private island in the Keys and the resort. Legendary in the hotel business, not least because its owner remained secretive. A recluse. No one even knew his name or how he had come to build one of the most luxurious resorts in the world.

She'd seen the layout in *Architectural Digest* and had marveled with everyone else at the Moorish, Arabian Nights fantasy that had been created. Sighed at the individual villas at the ocean's edge, at the private pools, the five-star restaurant, the fully equipped spa.

"Paradise," the brochure had said. "A place to escape to when it's time to be reborn."

Well, that certainly fit the bill.

"We'll be landing in about ten minutes," the pilot told her through her headphones, and she nodded. His crisp English accent was somehow comforting, like that of a businesslike nanny. Now that she was actually here, actually landing on Paradise, Alison felt a little insecure.

It had been daring, her business partner, Kate, had

reassured her, to take a vacation all by herself. Daring and adventurous. And also a chance to do nothing and just relax. Her last job had been planning a spring herb garden for a lakeshore estate, along with masses of brilliantly colored tulips to line the drive. She'd graphed out plans, ordered supplies, and put in sixteen-hour days. Relaxation sounded good.

This particular contest had been slightly different from others she had entered, where two, four, or even eight people got to share the prize. The rules had been very specific. The winner, and the winner alone, was given the free vacation. And it was longer than most five- and seven-day jaunts—a full ten days.

That hadn't bothered Alison. A contest junkie, she'd entered five other contests that day. She'd dropped the postcard into the mail, addressed to Florida, without a thought. This trip to Paradise had been only one of many contest prizes.

But in her heart, she'd wanted to win. She'd wanted long walks along a private beach, spectacular sunsets, a tropical drink in hand. She'd wanted to wear a brief little sundress, or nothing but a bikini, and feel the ocean breezes on her body. The weather in Illinois she'd left behind had been typical for July—hot and muggy. Well, Florida was reputed to be muggy, but she was an optimist. There were those tropical trade winds to cool a body off.

The helicopter began its descent toward the helipad, and Alison leaned forward for a better look.

The grounds were nothing short of magnificent. Manicured lawns, tropical flowers, palm trees with their fronds swaying in the wind. Her landscaper's eye briefly took in the bright riot of colorful blooms. Plants she had only seen in pictures came to vivid life; tall oleander bushes, frangipani and wild purple orchid trees. A royal poinciana, shading one side of the landing strip, looked like an enormous red umbrella. Vines seemed to climb everywhere, and a huge banyan tree sent out fat aerial roots over the manicured lawn.

Coconut and date palms looked like spiky green fountains, and brilliant red hibiscus blossoms almost seemed to glow in the hot sun. The landscape artist in her itched to get her hands on some of these plants, to watch them, see how fast they grew or how well. She thought of what it would be like to work in a lush Eden like this one, but before she could continue that pleasurable daydream, the pilot was speaking to her over her headphones, telling her a limousine awaited her arrival.

The noise of the propeller blades seemed deafening as she removed her headphones and gratefully took the hand of the man who had opened the passenger door and was assisting her.

Within minutes, she was stowed in a limousine, along with her luggage, and headed toward Paradise.

SHE'D ARRIVED BY NOW.

He paced the grounds of his kingdom, impatient. Wondering if this would work, wondering if she would want to talk to him again, or even see him. Their last parting had not been amicable, but bitter. Deeply bitter. They'd thrown words at each other designed to wound, and each mark had found its emotional target.

Now, he was creating a situation where she would have to face him. But would she?

He'd toyed with the idea of ordering everyone else off his island, of making it only the two of them, of trapping her here until he managed to get the truth out of her. He'd entertained that idea for the merest of seconds, then known he couldn't do it. It wasn't in his heart to do anything to frighten Ally. He didn't want to hurt her in any way. But the thought had been tempting, to force something to happen that he wasn't sure ever would.

His thoughts turned toward the practical. Should he give her the first day alone and a serene night's sleep? Or should he give her mere minutes in her room before he barged in and let her know the true reason for this vacation, this time out of time?

Should he attempt to woo her all over again? Court her? Or should he come sweeping in, demanding vengeance, demanding answers, forcing her to come to terms with what they had done to each other?

Flynn decided he had to see her first. Then, and only then, would he make his decision.

SHE STEPPED out of the limousine and into a dream.

The circular drive faced an open area, with high ceilings and open walls. Tropical birds could easily swoop through, and bright sunshine spilled over everything, making her squint and reach for her sunglasses.

The center of the ceiling was a circle, open to the brilliant blue sky, and Alison imagined rain pouring in during the stormy season. She glanced down and saw that the area was all tiled, an intricate Moorish design of blues and golds. A fountain also occupied this area, its delicate streams of water creating a soothing background sound. Sprays of miniature yellow orchids were clustered artistically in cobalt blue vases, and elegant orange and purple birds of paradise created stunning bouquets on lacquered end tables.

She felt as if she'd entered a harem.

"Would you like something to drink?" a smiling woman said, carrying a silver tray with several different types of fruit juices in crystal glasses.

"Thank you." Alison hesitated, then chose some fresh-squeezed pink grapefruit juice. She sipped it gratefully, still feeling the dehydrating effects of her flight from Chicago.

"You're all checked in," said a slender man named Brad. He had opened the limousine's door when she'd arrived, introduced himself and informed her that he was her personal steward, something like a butler. "Your luggage is already on the way to your villa. Would you like a ride in one of our golf carts, or would you care to walk?"

The flight had felt so restrictive, even though it had been first class all the way.

"I'd like to walk. I'd love to see something of the resort."

Brad smiled up at her, and Alison thought briefly of Flynn. He'd never had to look up at her; he'd been the perfect height. At five foot ten inches, she'd felt rather gawky most of her life.

"As you wish," Brad said, indicating that she should follow him. Alison took one last look around the lushly appointed lobby, then began her journey.

HE'D CAUGHT SIGHT of her and instantly felt she deserved a night of sleep. The Ally he'd known was all but absent. Her glorious caramel-colored hair, which he'd loved to see tumbled all around her shoulders, was firmly restrained in an elegant twist. The Ally he'd known, who'd lived in shorts, tops and simple sundresses, had been wearing an elegant suit. Even he, with his limited knowledge of fashion, knew it had to have cost the earth.

But it had been the tired expression on that lovely oval face, the tension around her mouth, the lines around her clear blue eyes that had shocked him. He'd used binoculars, spyglasses, to catch a glimpse of her, and had immediately honed in on her face. The laughing Ally, the sparkling Ally he'd fallen in love with, was all but gone. He'd seen her hand shake ever so slightly as she'd reached for the elegant crystal glass of juice. And Flynn watched her as carefully as he'd ever watched sky and sea for clues about upcoming storms.

What's happened to her?

For just an instant, he let himself imagine that she'd been pining for him, longing to see him again, feeling incomplete without his love. Flynn, though he hated to admit it, was something of a romantic. Yet there was a part of him that rebelled against those deep feelings. He wanted to be in control, because he'd learned from painful experience that to be out of control, especially with feelings, extracted far too high a cost.

He'd also always been a compassionate person. Sometimes it had cost him; more often it had served him in good stead. Now, watching the woman he loved walk away, he reacted less to the visual stimulation of those slender, swaying hips and more to the expression on her face, to the tiredness he'd practically felt himself.

Within the minute, he'd forcibly shaken himself out of his reverie and headed toward the kitchen. His next step in this master plan was to talk to the chef.

SHE'D NEVER LIVED this way in her entire life.

She'd grown up with money. Lots of it. But she'd

never seen opulence on this scale. She'd never had not one, but two maids unpack for her, carefully hanging up her clothing, carefully arranging her shoes in the closet and folding her other clothes in the dresser drawers.

She'd never had a Brad, a personal assistant-butler-steward-whatever, someone who reacted to her slightest whim. She'd never been so cosseted, cared for, pampered, in her entire life.

The phone rang, and though she was in easy reach of it as she sat on the incredibly comfortable white couch in the main sitting area and took all this in, Brad answered on the first ring.

"Yes. Yes, Miss Hennessy is settling in quite nicely. Oh. I see. I wasn't aware that this was part of the contest. It is? Oh. Very nice. Well, I'll let her know."

While Brad was talking, Alison opened the sliding glass door that led to her personal patio, with two comfortable chaise lounges, a private barbecue, an umbrella-shaded table surrounded by four chairs and her own personal lap pool.

Heaven.

"Miss Hennessy?"

She turned, slightly unnerved. "Alison is fine."

"Miss Alison. I have been informed that part of your prize winnings includes a dinner served in your room early this evening, as you may be tired from your flight down."

She hesitated. "Actually, that does sound pretty good."

"Splendid. Now, I'm assuming you've already had lunch, so would you desire a snack before dinner?"

"Perhaps something to drink," she said.

"The villa's refrigerator is fully stocked," he said,

starting inside. "If there's anything you want that you don't see, just give the kitchen a ring and ask for Wolfgang."

Unbelievable. "I certainly will."

"May I pour you some juice?"

She opened her mouth to reply, hesitated, then had the sudden intuitive flash that this man, Brad, would be hurt if she didn't allow him to do his job.

"What kinds of juices are available?"

"Orange, papaya, pineapple coconut, mango, guava, grapefruit, carrot, watermelon—"

"Pineapple coconut would be fine." Then, as an afterthought, she said, "Could you add some rum?"

"Even better, I'll use the blender and make you a piña colada."

The tropical drink was served to her in a frosted glass with a slice of fresh pineapple as a garnish. Alison kicked off her shoes and curled up in one corner of the couch, drink in hand.

"I'll leave you, then," Brad said quietly. "Just ring if you should need anything."

"I will."

He'd barely shut the door before she leaned back on the plush couch and, after enjoying and finishing the tropical drink, she closed her eyes, set her empty glass on the marbletopped coffee table and drifted off to sleep.

HE HAD TO SEE HER.

Flynn didn't know if he was behaving wisely or not, but he didn't particularly care. All he knew was that he had to see Ally, had to find out what was causing her such unhappiness.

He suspected it might be her family legacy.

From the beginning of their courtship, back in high school, Jim Hennessy had stood squarely in the middle of his daughter's happiness. In his opinion, Flynn hadn't been good enough for his cherished and only daughter. But Ally had had other opinions, and so had Flynn. They'd defied her father and had managed to marry and make it last for almost eight months.

As Flynn headed toward Ally's bungalow, he wondered why Jim had never really looked out for anyone's happiness but his own. He'd treated his daughter as if she were simply an extension of himself, without a thought of her own. Was that why she looked so exhausted? Was she still trying to placate and please everyone in her life?

He headed down the pathway toward the beach and the most expensive villas. They could have dinner together. The worst thing she might do was demand he leave, throw him out. He'd leave, but he'd be back the next morning. And the morning after that. And the one after that.

He let himself into her villa stealthily, listening the entire time.

Not a sound.

Quietly, without a word, he went through the two upstairs bedrooms with balconies that faced the sea, the huge walk-in closet and storage area and the elegant marble bathroom with its sunken tub. He'd let himself in the back door, which, as the villas were built on ground that dropped toward the shore, led to the second floor. Moving carefully so as not to make a sound, he made his way down the carpeted steps to the first floor, with the master bedroom, second bath, expansive sitting area, kitchen and patio.

Perhaps she'd decided to take a walk on the beach.

Flynn fervently hoped she'd cast aside that elegant suit for something more appropriate to the weather.

He peered around from the staircase, saw her and froze.

Fast asleep, Ally was curled up in a corner of the couch, using one of the brocade cushions as a pillow. Her hair had come undone and was as he'd always remembered it, framing her face, a riotous mass of waves.

Memories choked his throat, other times, moments when he'd come awake with her, when they'd shared a bed and a life and a love so strong he'd thought nothing in this world could take it away.

He'd learned that the world could be a cruel place.

He approached her slowly, not wanting to make a false move. Came to her side, knelt, studied her face. She breathed softly, her chest rising and falling. Flynn could smell the scent of rum on her breath, and he frowned. The Ally he'd known rarely drank alcohol.

Her lashes fluttered. She made a soft little sound of distress, then turned and burrowed into the couch's comfortable cushions, her skirt riding up slightly and showing an elegant expanse of leg.

Flynn swallowed, but kept staring at his wife.

Ex-wife, he reminded himself.

Wife.

He took in the slight smudges beneath her eyes, the pallor of her skin that diminished those beautiful features. She was working too hard, and the only time Ally worked too hard was when she wanted to escape her problems, evade her life. That part of her personality he knew all too well.

He sighed, then decided he would wait until morning. As he started to rise, Ally's eyelids fluttered again, then opened.

And then he was staring at her, face to face. The meeting he'd wanted for so long, the moment he'd planned for months, was finally at hand.

"FLYNN?" she said, the word barely a whisper.

She had to be dreaming. Alison had been thinking about her ex-husband just before she'd drifted off to sleep. It hadn't been the way she'd imagined spending these magical ten days, thinking of her ex, but she'd been so tired. Then the flight, everything so different and new, the exquisite villa by the ocean, the tropical drink—all of it had lulled her senses, enabling her to let her guard down and think of Flynn.

And now here he was, in her dreams.

"Flynn?" she said again, softly. He looked wonderful, as wonderful as any man looks in a dream. But rougher. Harder. The young man she'd loved and married had matured, but not in the way most men did. This man who knelt in front of her by the white sofa looked tan and muscular and—dangerous.

His thick, dark hair, which he'd worn slightly longer than most fashionable cuts, reached his shoulders, sun-streaked and untamed. His body seemed sculpted of muscle, no trace of softness, his skin deeply tanned. Dressed in a pair of cutoff jeans and a white shirt unbuttoned to the waist, he looked like a man from another age. He looked like a pirate in one of the historical romances she so loved, even to the small gold hoop in one ear.

If he'd held a cutlass between his teeth, the picture would have been complete.

Yet it was his eyes that held her attention. Clear,

bright and deep green, with a depth of feeling inside them that moved her. They caused all sorts of feelings she had no desire to feel to collect in her stomach and start to push their way to her heart.

Danger. This man was as dangerous to her as any pirate in days past.

"Flynn?" she said again, because she couldn't figure out what he was doing here, in her dream, invading her life, looking like a man capable of doing anything, depending on what he wanted.

He stroked her cheek, his touch very light, caressing her cheekbone. Then he stood, so quietly, so gracefully, and walked out the sliding glass door, past the billowing white sheer curtains, toward the sea.

THIS WAS GOING TO BE so much harder than he'd thought.

Flynn retreated to his private office and wondered what he was going to do next. He'd already blown it, breaking into her villa and watching her sleep, then waiting until she woke and even touching her!

Not good. Not good at all. He was out of control.

But he hadn't been able to resist. The way Ally had come awake, the sweetly puzzled look on her face, then the change of expression, to wonder, then longing, then—

Fear. He'd seen fear in those blue eyes, and he'd known, with a sick feeling in his gut, that he was the man who'd put it there. Oh, he'd never raised a hand to her and despised any man who thought that was any sort of answer. But the words they'd exchanged years ago had been harsh, both of them fighting for their emotional lives.

What would she do now? Would he go back to the

villa and find she'd packed her bags and headed north? Or had she thought he was a dream? Would she excuse seeing him as something brought on by exhaustion or an overactive imagination?

Impatient, he picked up his private line, punched a button.

"Has she checked out yet?" he said, the minute Brad answered the phone.

When Brad answered in the negative, Flynn let out the breath he hadn't even been aware of holding. Still here. She'd stayed. He didn't care why or how, he just knew he wanted another chance.

And this time, he wouldn't let his emotions get away from him.

ALISON WOKE, stretched, took in the fact that the sun was lower in the sky and wondered why she'd dreamed about Flynn.

Strange. He'd been kneeling by her couch, so when she'd looked at him, their eyes had been level. Then he'd reached out and touched her....

Her hand came up. Her fingers traced her cheekbone, following the path Flynn's touch had taken. Why had she dreamed about him? Why had she dreamed he'd touched her? And why did she still feel as if she craved his touch?

Nothing had been simple when it came to Flynn.

She'd been so young when she'd met him. A girl, really. And so many times, as their relationship had deepened over the years, she'd wished they'd met later, when she had a little more experience and wisdom. Flynn was not an easy, compliant man. But he'd been loyal, trustworthy, passionate, so vibrant, full of life and dreams—

Until the end, when it had all come crashing down.

He'd assured her that all he needed was a life with her, but she'd never felt up to the job. How could a man like Flynn have taken one look at her, *one look,* and decided she was the one he wanted forever? How did people make those decisions with such assurance?

Yet she had. One look at Flynn, and no one else, no other man had even existed for her. Which was why, after their divorce, there had been no one. Even though her father had paraded a succession of suitable men through his estate in Evanston directly after the divorce and hinted—none too subtly—that he was getting on in years and wanted a grandchild, preferably a boy if she could manage it, thank you very much.

No, she'd thrown herself into her work and matured more in the six months following her divorce from Flynn than she had in the previous six years. Her heart had turned to ice, and she'd resigned herself to a life alone, though she'd thought of adopting a child as the years went on. But marriage? Not for her. Her own had burned so brightly and passionately for such a short time. Another marriage, to another man? Unthinkable. It would be like trying to eclipse the sun.

Alison got up from the couch, stretched again, then headed for the bathroom. Once inside, she had to stop and simply stare at the Italian marble walls and tub, at the huge open shower stall, at the three pedestal sinks along the one huge, wall-length mirror, at the separate, enclosed bathroom stall.

Knowing that what she needed was a hot bath and an hour of sheer mindlessness, she turned on the taps full blast, squirted a generous amount of peach-scented bubble bath beneath the spray, then stripped off her clothing where she stood and climbed in. All her toiletries were unpacked and lined the large shelf above the sinks, but there were also generous bottles of shampoo, conditioner, body wash and moisturizer supplied by the resort. She reached for a bottle of shampoo, then ducked her head beneath the mounds of bubbles rapidly filling the massive marble tub.

Memories of Flynn or not, she was going to have a good time.

ALISON HAD just wrapped her hair in a thick towel and donned one of the terry-cloth robes supplied by the resort when she heard a knock on the door.

"Coming!" She belted the robe tighter around her waist, then raced barefoot to the sliding glass door overlooking her private patio, where a young man in khaki shorts and a coral-colored polo shirt held a huge silver tray.

"Dinner," he said as she opened the door.

She remembered Brad saying something about a complimentary dinner being part of the contest package and didn't say anything as he walked inside and placed the silver tray on the coffee table.

"Is there anything else I can do for you?"

She shook her head. "Everything looks great."

"Just ring us if you need anything." He exited through the sheer white curtains, which lifted and danced in the breeze let in by the open glass doors, though he had carefully closed the screen door behind him. Alison was glad of that—everyone in Illinois had been compelled to tell her about the huge bugs in Florida, and she wasn't a fan of sharing her living quarters with them.

Staring at the silver tray, she reached for the remote and clicked on the television. A news program was in progress, so she channel surfed until she found a music channel. Settling on to the comfortable couch, she lifted one of the silver lids.

Her hand faltered as she set the lid down. Curry. Not only curry, but her favorite Thai curry, shrimp and pineapple in coconut milk. A side of white rice, and a side of mixed vegetables.

Fate could be very cruel. For a moment, Alison flashed back in time, to a tiny Thai restaurant Flynn had found, a regular hole-in-the-wall, but the food had been to die for. He'd introduced her to Thai food, and she'd known then that he was an adventurer in every sense of the word.

Carefully, practically holding her breath, she lifted the other lids.

Vegetarian spring rolls with a pungent dipping sauce. And the most decadent chocolate brownie with raspberry sauce encircling it. A glass of iced water and a glass of very good white wine. She rarely drank, but when she had, it had always been white wine.

She frowned. Then the frown cleared as she remembered the call she'd received informing her she had won this vacation in Paradise. She couldn't quite remember, but perhaps during that blur of questions, she'd been asked several about her favorite foods. And it wasn't any stretch of imagination to include chocolate on any woman's plate.

Satisfied with her assessment of the situation, she picked up her fork and started to eat.

HE WATCHED HER from the beach. Not her, exactly, but he watched her villa. Flynn saw her come out to take in the glorious sunset the Keys were known for, the skies bathed in Technicolor oranges and pinks before the

sun sank into the Gulf. Then the clouds would glow
with rich color, the tourists would take their pictures,
and the whole affair would be over for the day.
Though he'd lived here for years, the sunsets never
failed to astound him. He'd watched many of them at
sea, after a hard day's work.

But now he had his eye on something—*someone*—
else.

He noticed that she'd changed into a brief bathing
suit, and Flynn speculated that Ally would probably
enjoy her private pool before retiring for the night. He
and Teddy stood on the beach, at the shoreline, and
watched the lights from the first floor of the villa.

"Tomorrow," he told his dog, ruffling the animal's
shaggy ears. "Tomorrow we'll go and see her."

And then… He had no idea.

Teddy whined, and his ears pricked. Flynn saw Ally
come onto the patio and lean against the railing. If she
walked down three cement stairs, she would be on the
sand, close to the shoreline.

Teddy whined again, his nose lifting in the wind,
and Flynn realized his dog had picked up her scent.
The Lab mix had had a strong bond with Ally and had
loved her passionately. She'd brought the little puppy
home their first Christmas and insisted he was the best
gift of all because Flynn had never had a dog. He remembered that awful weight of guilt in his chest when
he'd taken Teddy with him after the divorce. But Ally
had been nowhere to be found by the time he left Illinois. She'd taken flight, all rage and passionate anger.

Flynn reached to thread his fingers through his pet's
collar, then glanced down in horror when he realized
the dog was no longer there. Teddy was loping toward

Ally's villa, his tongue lolling out of his mouth, his feathery black tail waving madly.

Teddy was about to blow his whole plan.

Flynn put two fingers in his mouth and whistled sharply.

The dog ignored him, seemed to run faster.

Flynn watched, resigned. Sometimes it was better when fate took a hand in things. He knew that from experience. Hell, he hadn't even been sure he wanted to wait until morning to see her again.

Teddy had reached the cement steps and nudged the steel gate. The dog barked impatiently, and Flynn sighed, had to grin, then started up the sand.

SHE HEARD A DOG BARKING, and it brought her out of her thoughts. Startled, she glanced at the gate and saw the huge black dog, tongue hanging out of its mouth, enormous white teeth gleaming in contrast to its shiny coat, eyes bright with—

Recognition? Her throat closed. *No…*

It couldn't be. It couldn't. But the dog barked again, sharply, impatiently, as if saying, "You remember me, don't you?"

It had to be Teddy. Memories flooded back as she walked to the gate, unlatched it, let the enormous dog into her patio and fell to her knees, putting her arms around the massive neck and letting the animal revert to a delighted puppy as he covered her face with wet, doggy kisses.

Memories continued to assail her, the smell of their Christmas tree, the laughter as Flynn had realized that this impatient puppy had chewed halfway out of the artfully wrapped box she'd designed. Teddy had been wriggling his little puppy body so quickly that the en-

tire box had seemed to vibrate as she had handed it to
Flynn on Christmas Eve. The puppy had exploded out,
getting tangled in the bright red ribbon, and launched
himself at Flynn, covering his face with kisses as he
was doing to Ally now.

"Teddy," she whispered, hugging the dog tighter.

Teddy went into a rapture of dancing and wriggling,
licking and snuffling and whining. Then he broke loose
and began to race around the enclosed patio in circles,
barking and jumping and stopping each time he
reached her for another quick kiss.

She'd been so filled with joy at the sight of her dog
that the next thought hit her with tremendous emotional force.

If Teddy's here, then Flynn...

She turned and looked into the darkness, the silvery
sand, the ocean's shimmering surface turned to molten
quicksilver by the moon. Palm trees rustled in the
breeze; the scent of flowers filled the night air. And she
saw that gleam of white approaching, then made out
his shape, still in those cutoffs and that white shirt.
Barefoot, with his hair swirling around his shoulders,
he came closer. He started up the stairs, and she put
her hand to her throat, grabbed the railing for support.

Not a dream. Never a dream.

Then he was standing in front of her, mere feet away,
while Teddy, the dog they both loved, pranced delight-
edly between them. She didn't know what to say as she
studied the hard planes of his face, the muscular shoulders and finally looked into his eyes. From the reflection of the lights inside she could see his expression
was guarded. Observing. He watched her the way a
wild animal watched its prey.

Her throat closed, and she gripped the handrail

tighter. A terrible roaring started in her ears, louder than the waves below.

"Hello, Ally," he said softly.

She reached out, as if imploring him to be a dream, as if reality were simply too much to bear, then felt her knees giving way, Teddy barking, then strong arms around her and Flynn's muffled curse before darkness claimed her.

2

SHE WOKE with the feeling she was in a dream.

Darkness surrounded the villa, and even though Alison didn't glance at the bedside clock, she sensed she hadn't been out that long. Flynn had placed her on the queen-size bed in the villa's first-floor bedroom, then covered her with the folded blanket that had rested at the foot of the bed.

She stirred, restless, her eyes coming open, her senses assaulted.

Candlelight. Several candles had been lit and placed on the dresser beneath the large window that faced the ocean. Alison started to sit up, then stopped as she saw her ex-husband sitting in a chair directly across from her bed.

He wasn't a dream, not at all. But he wasn't the man she had divorced eight years ago. Flynn had changed, and as she studied him, she took the time to catalog those changes.

The man she had divorced had always been a rebel. He'd worn his hair a little longer, defied convention, questioned everyone and everything. He'd lived by a code of his own, independent and full of challenge. But there had always been a softness in his eyes, a kindness, when he looked at her.

Now, in the candlelight, she wasn't quite sure what she saw in those eyes.

His hair was long and thick, with a slight wave. The

sun had streaked the dark brown length of it, just as it had deeply tanned his face and the expanse of muscled chest she could see beneath his unbuttoned white shirt.

His features seemed more deeply defined, as if someone had carved his high cheekbones, squared jaw and strong nose from a fine-grained wood. Not an ounce of fat remained anywhere on his bone structure. It was as if sand and wind and surf had chiseled the man who sat in front of her. As if the elements had created him.

He looked like a pirate, down to the small gold hoop in his pierced ear.

She shifted beneath the covers, aware suddenly that she had nothing on but her brief, two-piece swimsuit. And that they were alone. Well, except for Teddy. The large black dog sat adoringly at Flynn's feet, looked at her and whined, then thumped his tail on the tile floor.

"Teddy," she said softly, and patted the bed. The dog crouched, then bunched his muscles and jumped on the bed, causing the mattress to dip alarmingly. Teddy had grown, had to weigh at least eighty-five pounds. She knew he was part Lab but had never quite figured out what the other part of his parentage was. Another large breed, to be sure.

The dog licked her face, then circled the bed and lay with his head in her lap. He gazed at her happily as she slowly stroked his head, scratched his ears.

Flynn said nothing, and because the silence stretching between them felt unbearable to her, Alison finally said, "Hello, Flynn."

Hello, Flynn.

This was not the way she'd imagined meeting him. Whenever she'd felt particularly bitter, she'd imagined meeting him at a party or in a bar, at a moment in her life when she looked utterly spectacular with not a care in the world. She'd wanted to meet up with him at her best, to show him she didn't need him in her life. To show him that she never had.

All lies, of course, but lies she could have lived with.

Never in her wildest dreams would she have chosen to meet Flynn in a bathing suit, lying in bed after fainting at his feet, knowing she had to look exhausted, her makeup smeared, not feeling her best. And while he looked disgustingly healthy, happy and whole.

He appeared to be holding all the cards. She simply had to make the best of it.

"Hello, Ally," he replied, and the sudden rush of heat that suffused her body shocked her. That voice. That deep, husky voice brought back so many memories, so many of them sexual. She only had to close her eyes to remember that voice in the dark, telling her how much he wanted her, what he wanted to do to her, how much he loved her—

She tensed beneath the covers, not wanting to remember.

"This is quite a coincidence," she said, feeling as if words were so inadequate. "You being here, I mean." She swallowed against the sudden tightness in her throat. "Are you taking some sort of vacation?"

"No." The single word was said softly, and for some reason it made Alison come to a state of full alertness. Something was not right.

"Flynn," she said, not wanting to anger him but needing to know the truth. "Are you…are you following me?"

"Not exactly."

She had to continue her questioning.

"Then what are you doing here?"

He seemed to hesitate for an instant, then said, "I brought you here."

It took a moment for the words to register.

"I...I don't understand what you mean."

"I arranged for you to come here."

"Here? But...there was a contest and—"

"It was rigged," he said. "You were supposed to win it."

She stared, her hand coming to a stop on Teddy's broad head, her entire body going very still.

"But...you couldn't have...there are laws—"

He laughed then, softly, and she watched him.

"Ally, don't you think that with enough money, those rules can be broken? Or at least modified."

"How did you—"

"I knew you loved to enter contests. I knew you would enter this one. It was a simple matter, finding your postcard and notifying you that you had won the prize."

It was all too much to comprehend. It didn't seem real. That he should go to all this trouble—and to what end?

As soon as she asked herself the question, she knew.

"Flynn," she said quietly, trying for as much composure as possible. "I want to leave. Now."

"And if I told you you couldn't?" He didn't say the words in a threatening way, but the quiet way he said them disturbed her even more.

"I'll call—" She thought for the fleetest of seconds. "Brad. Or...or Wolfgang."

"They both work for me."

Another shock assaulted her senses. "What are you talking about?"

He seemed to be studying her intently. "Paradise. I own it."

She stared at him, unable to take this all in. The Flynn she had known back in Illinois had been a hard worker, but his family had been far from rich. They'd struggled to stay afloat. And now Flynn owned Paradise?

Teddy whined, then butted his head against her hand.

"This?" She could barely get the word out. "This...all of this?"

"Yes."

"How?" She couldn't believe it, but maybe if he told her how he'd come to own this resort, she could.

"Buried treasure." He said the words with a smile, a smile that had once caused her heart to turn over and was making it beat rather rapidly right now.

"Buried treasure," she repeated.

"Buried treasure," he said. "Right after our divorce, I drove down here and hooked up with a few men who were treasure hunters. They needed a cook, I needed the work. The rest was up to fate."

"Buried treasure," she said again, feeling suddenly light-headed. "What kind of treasure?"

"A Spanish ship from the sixteenth century, loaded with gold. The captain decided to split it four ways, so I took my share and created this place."

Pieces of the puzzle began to click into place. Flynn had taken a degree in architecture in college; he'd always wanted to build things. The owner of the resort had always been something of a recluse, not wanting his privacy invaded. And she'd read something in the paper, in the Sunday edition of the *Chicago Tribune* about six years ago, about four men who had found incredible treasure in the Atlantic, centuries after this particular ship had sailed.

"*El Corazon de Oro*," she said softly.

"Very good," he said, nodding. "The Heart of Gold, as she was called. She wasn't a disappointment."

And I was. The thought flashed into her mind, but she bit her tongue before she could say the words out loud. Well, now that this particular mystery was cleared up, she had to ask him another question, had to keep talking as she took this all in and tried to figure out what she was going to do.

"Your parents?" she managed to ask. "Where—how are they?"

His features softened for an instant. "Dad retired early, and I bought him the boat he always wanted to live on. He and Mom have sailed all over the Caribbean. They're having the time of their lives."

She asked him briefly about his brothers and sisters and wasn't surprised to find that Flynn had put every single one of them through school, then helped them get started in various careers. It was just the way he was.

Finally, she could stall no longer and asked him the question that was burning on the tip of her tongue.

"What do you want?" That was about as blunt as she could manage.

He didn't hesitate. "The truth."

"About what?" But she already knew.

"About what happened."

Now, unbelievably, that same deep rage began to well up inside her, that same incredible hurt that had savaged her when she'd found him in bed with another woman.

"You know what happened." Her voice was so low, so soft with anger, she was surprised he could even hear it.

"No. I know what your father wanted to have happen. I told you, Ally—"

"No! My father had nothing to do with Suzanne—"

"Then why did he marry her?"

She'd never dreamed he would find out about that. It had disturbed her, the wedding that had taken place almost two years after Flynn had left town. But their divorce had followed three years later, and Suzanne Haines was not the sort of woman who chose to stay in touch. Alison had no idea where her ex-stepmother was.

But she could remember the feeling of opening that motel room door and seeing Flynn and Suzanne in that large bed, their arms and legs entwined.

How could anything like that have been staged? To admit that her father would go that far to make sure Flynn was out of her life was to admit he wasn't the man she'd always believed he was. And that was something she couldn't do. Especially now. Jim Hennessy had died quietly in his sleep almost two years ago.

"How convenient for you, now that my father is—"

"Dead. I know. And I'm sorry, Ally, but I can't ignore what he did to us."

"What *you* did to us!" She pulled the light blanket to her chin, trying to muster as much dignity as she could. "I'd like you to leave. Now."

"No."

As simple as that, he refused. She'd forgotten how Flynn Ryder played by no rules but his own.

She scooted up against the headboard, as far away from him as possible.

"Flynn, what is it that you want? And why don't you respect what *I* want?"

"I do. But Ally, I have to get to the truth and lay it all to rest."

"It's over."

"I don't think it is."

Just like that, he issued a challenge.

She didn't know what to do. Well, she did. She had to get him out of her room, out of this villa, because, unbelievably, she was beginning to have feelings for him again. First rage, then hurt, then something else, something she didn't want to examine too closely.

Alison knew Flynn wouldn't hurt her, wouldn't ever force her to do anything. But she also knew he was one of the most persuasive men on the planet, and she didn't want to allow him to talk her into anything.

"I'm walking to the lobby," she said quietly. "I'll wait by the desk until morning, and then I'm leaving."

"The contest rules specify you have to spend ten days here in Paradise," he reminded her.

"The contest was rigged, so that disqualifies everything," she said stiffly.

"Are you scared of being here with me, Ally?" he said, his voice soft.

Her temper flared at his easy confidence. "Not on your life."

"Then how about a little dare?" he suggested.

The temptation to hear him out was irresistible. "You're on."

"You stay the ten days. I don't come near you, I don't touch you, unless you ask me to—"

"—as if!"

"—and at the end of those ten days, if you still feel the same way about me, you walk out of here without a backward glance, and I never bother you again. Ever."

She wavered for an instant.

"I give you my word," Flynn said quietly.

"As if that's worth anything." This time she did see a flash of quick pain in those fathomless green eyes.

"I give you my word. I won't lay a hand on you."

"How about some conditions of my own?" she said.

"Go on." All his attention was focused intently on her.

"*If* I stay, and *when* I win, I get to take Teddy with me. And you never bother me again. Ever."

"Done. But you have to stay the full ten days."

"Fine," she said.

"Good," he answered.

"You're going to lose," she warned.

"We'll see."

"There's nothing to see about."

He got up, and she was engulfed in a wave of memory, the way he moved, the powerful masculine grace with which he did the simplest things.

"Teddy," he said quietly to the dog.

The Lab mix looked at him beseechingly.

"Ha! See, he already wants to stay with me. You just lost your dog."

Flynn smiled at her, and Alison had to fight to maintain her composure, for he was the sort of man who filled any room he was in.

"I'd like to stay with you, as well."

"Not fair."

He grinned. "I said I wouldn't touch you. I didn't say I wouldn't talk to you."

"I'd like you to leave now."

He laughed. "You'd better lock your doors."

She sat up straighter in her bed as he started out of the room.

"What's that supposed to mean, Flynn?" she called after him.

"Just lock them."

SHE DIDN'T SLEEP the entire night.

Once again, even though she knew better, she'd let her temper and her pride get the better of her. She'd been thinking of getting away from Flynn, away from his peculiar brand of persuasiveness, and what did she do? She went and agreed to a stupid bet, all because she couldn't bear for her ex-husband to think she couldn't resist him.

But the truth was, she couldn't.

Alison lay in bed, listening to the sound of the ocean and the wind, listening to Teddy's even breathing and occasional grunt. And she thought about Flynn and how they'd met.

She'd been fourteen to his eighteen when she'd first seen him. He was a senior while she was a freshman, and she hadn't thought she had a chance. Awkward and clumsy with the great spurt of height she'd attained over the summer, she'd felt all arms and legs next to the more sophisticated senior girls.

She'd been more at home with her head in a book or working with her grandmother in the garden. She'd never had to struggle with schoolwork, but being an only child, it was sometimes hard for her to socialize with others. Alison envied the easy camaraderie of her friends who had grown up with brothers and sisters. She always felt so tongue-tied, so self-conscious.

She also had difficulty getting to school on time, and the third time she was late for first period, she found herself in after-school detention. As she slid into her seat with a stack of books, she'd decided to attack her algebra, which she was absolutely hopeless with.

Her eyes had widened as she'd glanced up and seen Flynn Ryder saunter in. He'd walked down the aisle of desks and slid into the one directly across from hers.

"Hi," he said, and she felt her face flush a brilliant pink.

"Hi," she managed to croak in return.

"Flynn Ryder," he said, offering her his hand. As if she didn't know who he was, one of the most popular seniors at Evanston Township High School.

"Alison."

"Alison what?" he asked, his smile gently teasing.

"Oh. Hennessy."

"Alison Hennessy. Why haven't I seen you in any of my classes?"

She swallowed, suddenly nervous. "Because I'm a freshman."

"Oh."

And with that single word, she realized he'd thought she was older. And she'd also realized she wished she'd lied.

"Well," she said, knowing nothing more could come of their conversation. "I'd better get to my studies."

"What are you working on?"

"Algebra."

He laughed.

She screwed up her courage.

"Why are you laughing at me?"

"The way you scrunched up your nose. It's not your favorite subject, is it?"

"No."

"Why not?"

Briefly, haltingly, she told him of the way her father had moved around, the several different schools she'd attended before they'd settled outside Chicago.

"And in each school, we'd do a new sort of math, or skip it altogether, so now that I have to do all this stuff, I don't really know what it is I'm doing."

"You should get a tutor," he said. "Someone who could help you for about an hour a day after school. Or an hour before. Could you come in early?"

"Probably."

"Ask Mrs. Lundsted," he said, indicating the blond woman at the front of the classroom. "She'll hook you up with someone really good."

The following week, when she walked into one of the classrooms an hour before first period began, she found Flynn sitting behind the desk.

"What are you doing here?"

He couldn't conceal his grin. "I'm your new tutor."

OF COURSE, she developed a massive crush on him and thought she kept it fairly well concealed. And she was never late again.

He taught her algebra, caught her up in basic math skills, but did far more than that. After they finished their lessons for the day, they usually had about twenty minutes to talk. And talk they did, about everyone and everything.

"You don't look shy," Flynn said one spring morning. "I thought you were very cool and sophisticated that first morning I met you in detention."

"Really?" The thought brought her tremendous pleasure.

"I did. You looked so graceful, walking down the hall."

She'd never thought of herself as graceful. Seeing herself through Flynn's eyes, she started to gain some confidence.

She shared her deepest feelings with him, including her longing for sisters and brothers.

"Your parents don't want any more children?" he asked.

"My mom died when I was seven."

"That's tough."

"I remember her in bits and pieces. Gram took care of me, though."

"And your dad?"

"Well, he works all the time." She eyed him. "What do your parents do?"

"Mom works at a coffee shop, and Dad is in construction."

"But who's at home?"

"I am. And Elaine, my oldest sister."

"So you watch over the other five." She knew Flynn was one of seven children, and his family sounded wonderful to her.

"Yeah. We watch out for each other."

She envied him that.

Several mornings later, Flynn shocked her by asking her to the prom.

"Me? Why?"

"Because I like you," he said simply.

"You don't have a girlfriend?"

"Well, you're a girl and a friend, so I guess you qualify," he teased.

"You know what I mean."

"No," he said. "I don't."

She studied him, wondering about this new turn of affairs in their relationship. "You're sure? I mean, all we ever talk about is algebra."

"Ally, we talk about a lot more than that."

The way he said her name, Ally, thrilled her. But she was far too shy to let him see how he affected her.

"Let me think about it," she said.

SHE ASKED Gram to catch the train into Chicago with her and help her pick out a dress. And she told her all about Flynn.

"How about this one?" she asked her grandmother. They'd made their way through several stores and were in one of Chicago's oldest and finest, Marshall Fields.

"Black is too draining a color for you," her grandmother said. "Darling, don't try to grow up too fast."

"But I don't want to look like a baby!"

"But you're only fifteen."

Her grandmother had given her permission to go to the prom with Flynn, but only if she could meet him. Alison had said of course. She took off the slinky black dress and reached for one of the softest, palest green.

"I like that, it goes with your hair."

And Alison liked it the moment she put it on. Cut on the bias of a shimmering, clinging material, it was a knockout of a dress, simple and sophisticated at the same time.

"Shoes, too, I think. And a bag. And you'll need to get your hair trimmed—" She stopped in midsentence as Alison gave her a fierce hug.

"Thank you, thank you, thank you!" she whispered against her grandmother's soft, wrinkled cheek. "You'll like him, I know you will."

Her grandmother did like Flynn, and Alison's first prom had been magical. Yet he didn't even kiss her, but escorted her to her door at a rather early hour, compared to what other couples were doing.

Alison made a point of not showing how hurt she felt. They were just friends, weren't they?

FLYNN LAY in his large bed in his suite at the resort. For some reason, he kept thinking about Alison and their first dance together, at his senior prom. She'd worn some kind of green dress, and it had been all he could do to keep his hands off her. She was fifteen, he was eighteen, and those three years between them had created a gulf he couldn't cross.

He'd met her grandmother the night he picked her up. Apparently her father had been away on business, and that was just fine with Flynn. Another man might not have been as easy to fool. Just friends, indeed. Yet he'd seen the expression in her grandmother's eyes, and she had seen too much. But she hadn't seemed to mind. She'd just given him a long, unwavering look that had said it all. *Take care of my little girl. Love her as much as I do, and everything will be fine.*

She'd seen right through him.

That year's theme had been King Arthur's court, a regular Camelot. When his friends had been ready to leave, to whisk their dates to the hotel rooms they'd booked for the all-night parties that were standard prom fare, he'd taken Ally out to dinner, to a romantic restaurant with a spectacular view of Lake Michigan. When they had talked a little too long, he made sure she went to call her grandmother and tell her they would be a little late, but they'd been in a restaurant the entire time.

He got her home safely, delivered her to the loving arms of her grandmother, then walked to his car, smiling the entire way.

He kissed her on her sixteenth birthday, after he took her out to dinner and gave her a gold bracelet that had cost him a month's salary.

Ally had been the reason he hadn't gone that far away to school. That and his family. The Ryder family had always just managed to squeak by. With both parents working blue-collar jobs and seven hungry mouths to feed, times had sometimes been tough. Flynn had held down a job from the time he was fourteen.

Getting ready for college, Flynn was smart enough to win a scholarship. Northwestern University in Chicago wasn't all that far from Evanston. He could drive in and see Ally every weekend. In a way, it worked out very well, being able to concentrate fully on his studies during the week, but saving his Saturdays for Ally, and most of his Sundays, as well. And of course, they spent hours on the phone.

They never seemed to run out of things to talk about.

Somewhere in the course of their relationship, they talked about marriage. It had come up so naturally, Flynn hadn't even questioned it. When Ally was eighteen, they would marry.

She also told him that she believed in marriage very strongly, and wanted to wait until they were married before they consummated their relationship. He respected her beliefs, but it became harder and harder for them to stop as things became steadily more passionate.

Flynn finished college, and Ally graduated from high school. Then her father dropped the bombshell—

he didn't want his daughter to get married before she finished college. He wanted her to get a fine education—"understand all of her options," was the way Jim Hennessy put it.

Flynn knew instinctively he was not one of the options in Ally's life her father approved of. But he was close enough to Ally's grandmother to talk to her about it.

"It puts my granddaughter in a horrible position," the older woman told him. "She loves you both so much. You have to understand, Flynn, Jim is her only parent, and she wants to please him. She reminds me so much of my daughter. They're softer people, and not often able to stand up for themselves or believe the worst in the people they love."

"Do you think he's right?" Flynn said.

"I think you're right for each other, and that's all that matters. Would you stand in the way of Alison getting an education?"

"Never."

"Well, you know that and I know that, but Jim doesn't want to know it. If you make her choose, Flynn, you'll cause her terrible pain. You'll tear her apart."

"What if he comes up with another excuse when she finishes her degree?"

Alison's grandmother had smiled softly. "I may not be around by that time. If Jim pulls any of his tricks, you go on and elope. Take my girl away from him if you have to, Flynn. But be careful. Jim's not a man who likes his plans thwarted."

THOSE WORDS HAD haunted Flynn in the years after the divorce. How he could have underestimated Alison's father still frustrated and angered him. But as the old saying goes, hindsight is always twenty-twenty.

Alison went to the University of Chicago and received her degree in three years instead of four. Her grandmother did indeed pass away. And her father tried to stop their wedding once again.

So Flynn did what any male in his situation would have done. Tried to the end of his patience, he kidnapped a willing Ally and stole her off to Mexico, where they were married and had a ten-day honeymoon in a romantic little village by the sea.

And every sensual dream he'd ever had came true during those ten days. For if Ally had wanted to wait until they were married, once she had made her vows, she became totally passionate and willing in his arms. And he was enough of an arrogant male to be proud of the fact that he was her first lover, and determined enough to insure he would be her last.

They'd flown home, and that was when Flynn had made his greatest tactical error. He'd underestimated the lengths Jim Hennessy would go to insure that his daughter's marriage ended in divorce. He'd never dreamed that his father-in-law would hurt his only daughter so deeply, almost destroy her emotionally, in order to get his own way and find her a man he deemed suitable for her to spend the rest of her life with.

One night several months later, Suzanne had come on to him in a bar. He'd been there because one of his younger brothers, Bryan, had been playing in a band, and Flynn had shown up to give his sibling some support. Suzanne had found him, bought him a drink, and the next thing he knew, he was opening bleary, drug-blurred eyes and staring into the horrified face of his wife.

Before he could explain anything, Jim Hennessy had whisked his daughter away, taken her to a place where he couldn't find her. The next time he'd heard from Ally, it had been when she'd served him with divorce papers. He'd written her an impassioned letter, but nothing had come of it.

The papers had been served again. He'd tried to find her, written another letter, telling her that he didn't remember making love to Suzanne, despite what the older woman told Ally.

Another silence, aided and abetted by her father, no doubt.

Finally, the third time, he'd signed the papers. Then he'd taken Teddy and everything else he possessed except the one woman he'd ever wanted, packed his car and hit the road. He'd driven until he'd come to Florida, all the way down to the Keys, until he couldn't drive any farther.

He'd found himself sitting in a bar, and then he'd hooked up with Shaun Brannagan, captain of the *Nemo*. Flynn had hired on to search for gold, gold from the days that pirates roamed the Keys, wrecking and then salvaging ships. They'd found it, that one-in-a-million chance, that stroke of fate that had completely changed his life. He'd taken his share and built this resort, and now his ex-wife was sleeping in one of his villas next to the ocean.

He'd waited for Ally to grow up, and that had been hard. He'd fought her father, and that had been harder still. Flynn had braved water and wind, storms that could destroy a man's soul, in order to find that gold. He'd signed aboard with a kind of death wish, not really wanting to go on if he couldn't share his life with Ally. Then he'd found more treasure than he could spend in a lifetime. Life could be deadly ironic.

But now he was facing the greatest challenge of his life.

He had exactly ten days to make his wife want to make love with him again. To love him again. And if he couldn't win this particular battle, he didn't know what he would do with the rest of his life.

3

ALISON WOKE UP with a sense of unreality as everything that had transpired the night before came flooding back. What kind of trick was this her exhusband had chosen to play on her? A rigged contest? Ten days at a resort, during which time she would be begging him to make love to her, to reconnect with a life that had ended eight years ago?

What bothered her was why she'd agreed to it. If she were well and truly finished with Flynn, why hadn't she walked out that door? Why hadn't she been stone cold emotionally, able to look him straight in the eye and tell him to go to hell?

Because she wasn't done with their relationship, either. Flynn wasn't the only one who wanted to get to the truth. Alison had spent so many sleepless nights staring at the ceiling, her mind and heart in agony. What had gone wrong? Why had the magic ended?

She had her secret thoughts.

The age difference had always bothered her. Four years might not seem like a lot to most people, but when she was just entering high school and Flynn was finishing his time there, it made a difference. She'd made it a point to find out as much as she could about this man she'd had an enormous crush on, and what she had heard had affirmed her instinctual sense that Flynn, while not a callous player, definitely had more sexual experience than she did.

She'd wanted to wait. She'd wanted to come to him a virgin, start her marriage with the intention of never sharing that part of herself with anyone else. But in the back of her mind, Alison had always wondered if she were enough for Flynn.

She'd never considered herself sexy. Gawky, yes. Coltish and clumsy, yes. But graceful, sensual, alluring, sexy, charming—no. She'd gone into therapy for a time after the breakup of her marriage, and one of the things she'd learned was that part of the reason she didn't have a whole lot of confidence with the opposite sex was that her father hadn't been around for a great part of her life.

She'd asked Gram about that once, when she was thirteen, and her grandmother had looked at her and smiled. But there had been a sadness in her clear blue eyes.

"You look so much like your mother," she'd said. "Though I don't think your father even realizes it, I think he avoids you at times because you remind him of her."

She knew her parents had been a love match, just as she knew her mother's death at such an early age had devastated her father. Her only comfort at her father's funeral was that her parents were finally together. She'd sat in that hard folding chair by the grave site and wondered if her father had loved her mother as much as she had loved Flynn....

Teddy stirred on the bed beside her, all eighty-something pounds of dog leaning against her. He grunted, snuffled, then turned over and began to cover her face with wet doggy kisses.

She had to laugh. Their pet was totally incapable of hiding his feelings, and he was clearly delighted to see her, delighted that the two people he loved most in this world were together again.

"Not together," she admonished him as she got out of bed and walked toward the opulent bathroom.

After another bubble bath, she changed into a brightly colored sundress with a green and orange pattern, then went to raid the refrigerator. She didn't feel like calling room service. She was surprised to hear a knock on the door as she was drinking her morning glass of orange juice.

Brad was at the door, a silver tray in hand.

"But I didn't—"

"It's all part of the package," he informed her, and as she followed him to the table in the downstairs sitting area, she wondered if he knew about her true relationship to Flynn. It didn't seem likely. Her ex had always been an extremely private person.

She stared at the tray as he swept off the lid. A gorgeous array of white and dark chocolate-covered strawberries graced a china plate. Behind Brad, another man entered with a chilled bottle of extremely expensive champagne in an ice bucket.

"Not the usual breakfast, is it?" Brad remarked with a twinkle in his dark eyes. "But then again, this is your vacation."

For one awful moment, she was tempted to ask him to take the entire lot back where it had come from. Flynn, seducing her with food. Her favorites, and foods she'd shared with him during happier times.

"I'm also to tell you that a massage has been arranged for your enjoyment this morning," Brad said. He and the other man turned to leave.

A massage sounded quite wonderful. Anything to

relieve the low level of tension that had pervaded her body since her awareness of Flynn being on this island.

"Should I go to the spa? At what time?"

"Oh, no," Brad replied. "The massage table has been set up on the beach, right on the shoreline. If you walk down to the ocean and turn right, you'll see it."

"An outdoor massage?" She hesitated. How could she take her clothing off outside, with other guests around? She wasn't a prude, but she wasn't that daring, and she voiced her thoughts to Brad.

The young man seemed genuinely confused. "I thought you knew. For the ten days you're our guest, you're our *only* guest at Paradise."

He departed in a flurry of efficiency, leaving her to stare at the strawberries. Her vision blurred, she was so angry.

You're our only guest at Paradise....

The sneak. Trust Flynn to slip that little detail right by her. And here she'd thought their ten days together would be so easy, with other resort guests to buffer the intense feeling between them. It would be easy to avoid Flynn in a crowd. One on one, she wasn't as confident.

Alison threw herself on the couch and eyed the bottle of champagne. Her first instinct, that this place reminded her of a harem, had been right on the mark. Flynn seemed to be setting up a masterful seduction.

Why? He claimed to be after the truth, so what would he gain out of forcing an intimacy she didn't want?

The flush that crept up her face told her she was lying to herself. She'd been thinking about Flynn in a most sensual way since she'd first seen him, a slow burn that continued to grow. If she'd thought he was beautiful that first day they'd met in detention, he was a gorgeous specimen of a man now. There was a wildness about him that hadn't been a part of his makeup before, and she wondered what that wildness would be like in bed....

Teddy, standing in the doorway of the bedroom and staring at her with his dark doggy eyes, whined.

"Don't worry, I'm not going anywhere." She patted the couch next to her and invited her beloved pet to jump up beside her.

"No chocolate for you, it's bad for dogs," she said, plucking a berry from the china plate and biting into it. The fruit, succulent and sweet, contrasted sharply with the dark, almost bitter chocolate. A very fine chocolate. Paradise was a first-class resort all the way.

Alison glanced at the champagne, a sneaky plan beginning to form in her mind. She got up, uncorked the bottle, found a glass in the kitchen and made herself a mimosa, half champagne and half freshly squeezed orange juice. Then she sat on the couch, ate another strawberry, took a long sip of her drink and scratched Teddy right behind his ears, just where he liked to be scratched.

Flynn was obviously counting on her being upset at being alone with him. That would be the perfect response from the old Alison, the virginal, young, innocent woman she'd been. But eight long years had passed since she and Flynn had divorced. Surely she had changed?

Actually, she hadn't changed all that much, except to have hardened her heart a bit. If she wasn't the same naive girl who had believed in happy endings, who could blame her? For all Flynn knew, she could have had a few wild flings of her own. *Many* flings. She could have been one of those women who went totally wild after their divorce and had several quick affairs they chalked up to post-divorce madness.

Perhaps she could play a part, a part that would help her get through the next ten days and safely off Flynn's island with her heart intact.

You can do this…

It wasn't as if the culture wasn't saturated with sex. All a person had to do was turn on the television, and there it was. Or go to a movie. Or turn on the nightly news. Alison had nothing against sex, for Flynn had been the kindest and most sensual of teachers. But she had the strongest desire to even up the playing field a bit.

She reached for another strawberry, bit into it.

Better and better…

Before she lost her nerve, she reached for the phone. Within minutes, she was connected with the gift shop. She asked the woman if there was any way a few select items could be brought to her room.…

SHE SAUNTERED DOWN the beach clad in a silk pareo, a turquoise, white and pink confection that skimmed her body like a cloud, the tropical trade winds molding it to her breasts and hips. The only other clothing she wore was a racy little black G-string and the cutest pair of flipflops. The woman at the beachwear boutique had warned her that she could walk barefoot on the sand but had better not try entering the water barefoot, as the ground underneath could be quite rocky and diffi-cult to navigate without protection.

Alison had thought the Florida Key's beaches would have finely grained white sand, but the sand seemed slightly coarse. Wilder, less tame. She'd read in the guidebook she'd brought along that to create finely grained sand you needed the constant pounding of surf, and the large bodies of water surrounding the Keys didn't put that kind of pressure on the islands.

Her eyes scanned the beach for shells. She had quite a collection at home from the summer vacations she'd taken with her grandmother. She noticed small white clam shells and a shell that looked like an upside-down snow cone. The best shells only came up on the beach after a storm, and the only storms she anticipated while at Paradise were the ones she and Flynn would create.

As she approached the massage table, she noticed there were two of them, and a secretive little smile curved her lips. Oh, how lucky she'd been that Brad had let slip she and Flynn were alone on his island resort except for select members of his staff. The old Alison, the Alison she didn't dare let out, would have thrown a little fit, would have been totally embarrassed and self-conscious at the thought of being naked outside, being naked with Flynn anywhere in view. But now she had another perspective on the battle of wills they were about to engage in, and she wanted to make him suffer.

She wanted to make Flynn suffer for taking Suzanne to bed. For every horrible emotion she, Alison, had felt as she'd slowly opened that motel room door.

"Hello," she said brightly. "You must be Hans."

The masseur looked up. He could have been a poster boy for a bodybuilding class, muscles upon muscles upon muscles. He had white-blond hair and icy blue eyes. Clad in a brief black spandex swimsuit, he seemed the sort of man who could pick her up with one beefy hand and break her in two. Then he smiled at her, those eyes warmed up, and Alison knew she was in good hands.

He'd been working on Flynn. The only reason Alison didn't stare, didn't completely lose her composure at the sight of her ex-husband, oiled and naked except for a brief white terry towel over his buttocks, was that she'd assumed he would already be here enjoying a massage or would somehow contrive to walk along the beach and be there while she had hers. She knew Flynn's modus operandi now, and clearly part of it was that he wanted to unnerve her, catch her off guard.

Forewarned was forearmed.

All's fair....

"Where would you like me, Hans?" she asked, looking at him. She'd deliberately lowered her voice, making the simple question sound a great deal more provocative than the straightforward words warranted.

Flynn frowned. She caught her ex's expression out of the corner of her eye and inwardly smiled.

Round one to Alison...

"Here on the table," Hans said, gesturing to the other massage table that had been set in the shade of a mangrove tree near the shoreline.

"All righty, then." Without a second's hesitation, she slipped off her beach shoes, then unknotted her pareo. The sheer silk slid off her body in a sensuous whisper, and she resisted the urge to hold it up in front of her breasts. Instead, she asked Hans another question.

"Where should I put this?" She held the brief wisp of silk out in front of her.

"Beneath the table," he said. His inspection of her was impersonal, and Alison was secretly grateful for his discretion. She didn't know if she could have dealt with a strange man ogling her nearly naked body.

She could feel waves of tension coming off Flynn, and that gave her the strength to do what she did next.

"Does this need to come off?" she said, hooking her finger beneath the lacy G-string and giving the elastic a frisky little snap against her hip.

The complete and utter silence from Flynn's table spoke volumes. She almost laughed out loud but bit the inside of her cheek. To laugh would have been to give up her ruse, and she wasn't quite ready to do that. Not yet. Maybe not ever.

"Up to you," Hans said. "I can work on your body much better if there is no restriction, no confining clothing at all. But if you are uncomfortable—"

"Not at all." Where she got the nerve, Alison never knew. But after all, Flynn had seen everything there was to see, and Hans was about as clinical as a doctor. With slow, deliberately seductive movements, she slid the G-string down her hips and over her legs. Then she stepped out of the brief scrap of black lace, grabbed it with her toes, kicked it up and caught it as if she did this little striptease every day of the week and twice on Sunday. Placing it with her pareo on the shelf beneath the table, she decided on one last little tease especially for Flynn.

Whereas the old Alison would have leapt for the table, racing to lie facedown, hoping the white towel would cover her butt, the new Alison, the Alison she was determined to be for as long as she was on this island, hooked her fingers above her head and stretched head to toe.

"This sunshine is glorious," she murmured, fully aware of how her breasts were lifting, her buttocks tightening. She found she enjoyed the cool, clean ocean scented air against her naked skin.

Maybe this adventurous approach to life isn't such a bad thing.

Then, taking her time, she got on the massage table and stretched out, groaning with appreciation as she lay facedown on the sunwarmed surface.

"Oh, this feels so good, Hans, and we haven't even started yet."

She didn't dare look at Flynn as she rested her face on her folded arms, hiding her smile.

HIS PLAN was backfiring. Badly.

Just as he'd underestimated Jim Hennessy, he'd underestimated Alison.

He'd assumed that time had stood still since the last day he'd seen her. Now, for the first time, Flynn realized she'd had a life of her own for the last eight years.

A life that might have included several love affairs.

The thought of her in another man's arms, moving beneath him, making those same little sounds in the back of her throat that used to drive him to his own completion, enraged Flynn to the point where he almost got off the table, grabbed her, flung her over his shoulder and carried her, stark naked, to his suite, to his private sanctuary, to his dark, shaded bedroom.

But sanity returned with the blink of an eye, and he realized he was a twentieth-century man and not some pirate taking a woman captive.

Though the way he was feeling, that captive idea didn't sound so bad.

He hadn't kept an eye on her the past few years. Flynn hadn't felt he had the right to do that, to invade her privacy so completely. But when he'd thought up this contest scheme, he'd hired a private detective to find her. That was how he'd discovered her father had passed away, and that Suzanne had divorced him a few years earlier.

In a totally irrational fit of male possessiveness, he wished he hadn't played by anyone's rules but his own. Flynn wished he'd had her followed the entire time after their divorce, that someone had observed all her activities and had warned him if another man had dared to show his face.

The thought of her with anyone but him was physically painful, and before he was aware of it, he let out a low moan.

"Flynn?" Ally raised herself off the massage table with one elbow, giving him a generous glance at her breasts. He'd always thought they were beautiful breasts, perfectly suited to her graceful frame.

"Is anything wrong?" she asked. She seemed genuinely concerned, but he couldn't be sure.

"Nothing at all."

"But you made a sound. It sounded like—"

"A muscle cramp. Hans, would you see to it?"

"Of course."

Flynn indicated his lower left leg, and Hans went to work with his magical hands. Flynn couldn't turn away. To avoid looking at Ally would be perceived as a sign of weakness. He couldn't have that.

"So," he said, "you've obviously had massages before." That would account for her new ease with her naked body and the way she had shown absolutely no embarrassment in front of Hans.

She considered this. "No, I can't say that I have. This is a brand-new experience for me, Flynn, and I do want to thank you for giving it to me."

He studied her face, sure there was a mixed message there somewhere, a double entendre, but he couldn't be sure.

"Hans is adorable, don't you think?" she whispered.

He couldn't believe his ears. His Ally, going gaga over this muscle-bound Neanderthal? Though Flynn usually had an excellent working relationship with Hans, whose magical hands could keep his headaches at bay after a long day at work, he looked at his employee in a new light. If Ally became attracted to Hans, his whole plan went out the window.

Everything had gone wrong. Hans finished with his leg and gave it a soothing pat. Flynn watched as the muscled mountain of a man turned his attention to Ally. As Hans oiled his hands and placed them on Ally's bare skin, Flynn felt the ugliest of emotions, utter and complete jealousy, erupt deep within him.

Yet there was nothing he could do.

THE MAN'S HANDS were magical, no doubt about it.

"Ahhh," Ally moaned, letting out tension with the long, drawn-out breath. "Oh, Hans, I can't *tell* you how *good* this feels."

She hoped she wasn't overdoing it. Alison didn't even have to glance in Flynn's direction. She knew her ex-husband in ways only a wife could, and at the moment he was not a happy camper.

It amused her, how she'd been able to see through his plan. He'd obviously thought to catch her off guard, but she'd managed to turn the situation in her favor. And the massage wasn't bad, either.

Oh, she'd had massages before at spas. But only in the privacy of a room, and most of the masseusses had been women. This massage, for which she was glori-

ously naked in the midst of nature with Hans the Bar-
barian, was a whole new experience, she had to admit.

"How long are you going to be with us, Alison?"
Hans inquired.

She could almost hear Flynn gritting his teeth and
was very careful to keep the laughter out of her voice.

"Ten days. Ten glorious days. I'm looking forward
to every single one."

"That sounds very nice," Hans said as he worked on
her legs. "You know, you have a beautiful body."

She didn't dare look in Flynn's direction, simply
heard the soft curse and smiled.

"Thank you."

"Seriously, you have no cellulite, and your skin is
quite lovely."

She knew Hans wasn't coming on to her, wasn't ha-
rassing her or trying to be offensive. He had an aesthe-
tician's appreciation of the human body.

"I try. I eat pretty well and I—well, I've found various ways to exercise outside the structure of a gym."

"*Ja*, that's the way to go. Do what you like, and the
body will follow, will show its appreciation."

Hans unwittingly played the part of a straight man
to her little comedy routine. She hoped Flynn found it
particularly irritating.

"Oh, I do what I like, all right."

She decided to close her eyes and enjoy the massage.
It was the safest option, because she hadn't been prepared for the sight of Flynn's naked body and the way
it made her feel. He'd been strong and fit when they'd
married, and she had wonderful memories of their
honeymoon in Mexico and the physical side of their
marriage before infidelity had reared its ugly head.

But it seemed as if Flynn had metamorphosed into

someone entirely different, almost a stranger. There was a new toughness about him, a lean, battle-scarred quality. If she didn't know any better, her fanciful imagination would have gotten the better of her and she would have thought of him as a pirate.

His time at sea had hardened him. She'd noticed the slight scar by his chin, a scar she'd never seen before. He seemed more muscular, not as muscle-bound as Hans, but his arms and legs were roped with the kind of muscle a man didn't get in the gym. These were the muscles of a man well used to hard, physical labor on a daily basis. She wondered at this, at why he hadn't gone all soft once he'd taken his money and become the owner of this resort.

The combination of everything about Flynn, the long sun-streaked hair, the sun-bronzed skin, the wariness in those deep green eyes, the toughened musculature of his body—she found herself so attracted to him. She felt as if she were falling for Flynn all over again, and even more than before.

And that couldn't happen if her plan was to work. This time, she didn't want to be the one who was duped, who was lied to and left in the dust. This time, pride demanded that she had to be the one to leave him, and Alison was determined that this ten-day idyll in paradise should end exactly that way.

She was so lost in her thoughts she almost didn't realize the massage was over.

"Well, I hope you enjoyed it," Hans said. At the sound of his voice, she realized he was packing away the various bottles of oils and lotions. While she, naked as the day she was born, with only a small white terry towel over her butt, lay on the massage table and felt as if her body had turned to butter. And that butter was presently melting in the tropical sun.

"Wonderful," she murmured.

"Ally," Flynn said. "If you lie outside much longer, you might burn."

"Mmm." She considered this. "Hans, would you be a dear and carry me back to the villa? I swear, I can't move a muscle."

The silence from Flynn's table was truly deafening.

"*Ja*, I can do that," said the masseur, and he handed her a thick white terry-cloth robe. "Just belt this around you, and I'll take you there."

Acting abilities she hadn't even known she possessed prevented her from laughing out loud at the look on her ex's face. Flynn's green eyes were murderous, and she wondered for an instant if she'd finally pushed him too far.

A part of her didn't care.

She got off the table, belted the terry robe around her waist, then stuffed the G-string in one of the robe's pockets. Grabbing her pareo and beach slippers, she looked at Hans, hoping her expression rivaled that of a child getting to go on a particularly exciting ride at Disneyland.

"I'm all ready," she announced brightly.

"I'll take her, Hans," Flynn said. He'd knotted the white terry towel around his waist, and his tone of voice, the gleam in his eyes, dared the other man to challenge him.

This is interesting....

"Whatever you say, boss," the huge man said complacently. He went back to gathering up his lotions and oils. "I'll return the tables to the spa."

"Fine." That one word came out of Flynn's mouth

clipped and abrupt. And Alison was barely prepared for the way she felt as he came around to her table and reached for her.

"You know," she said, quickly darting out of his reach, "I think that little bit of light-headedness has left me, and I can make it back to my villa on my own."

"I'll walk with you," he said.

"Whatever," she replied, trying to inject into her tone just the right amount of could-not-care-less attitude.

They walked in total silence until they reached the gate that led to her patio and lap pool. She turned to face him, determined to appear composed. Cool and serene, a woman who dealt with these sorts of things on a daily basis.

"Flynn, thank you so much for the—"

"Have dinner with me."

Not a question, but an order. How like Flynn, now that he'd been slightly taken aback by her little performance.

"Dinner? Here? Tonight?" She put the words up as a shield as she tried to collect her thoughts and come up with her next plan of attack.

"Dinner. Here. At The Reef," he said, referring to the five-star restaurant on the resort's grounds.

"What time?" she asked, striving for a casual attitude.

"Eight."

She smiled at him and had to physically restrain herself from reaching up and touching the scar on his chin, caressing the side of his face. "Sounds like fun. We can talk about old times."

The slight movement in his jawline, the faintest tic of a muscle, fascinated her. She was getting to him, she really was. The knowledge filled her with a heady sense of feminine power.

"I'll pick you up at eight," he said, staring at her as if they'd never met. *And indeed*, she thought, *he's never met this side of me.*

She stretched, and knew his gaze was on the front of her terry robe where it gaped alarmingly, revealing cleavage, almost exposing a nipple.

"Great." She yawned for effect. "That gives me plenty of time to go to bed, take a little nap and then a hot, hot bath." She paused, then said, "I'll meet you there, Flynn. Bye."

She turned and unfastened the gate's latch. Knowing his eyes were on her every inch of the way, she sauntered—there was no other word for it—to the sliding glass doors and let herself inside. Then, because she knew his eyes were still on her, she loosened the terry tie on her robe and let it slide off her and pool at her feet. She stretched sinuously, every tiny muscle, giving him a view of her naked backside, still gleaming with massage oil, before padding barefoot to her bedroom.

Inside, she locked the bedroom door, then raced to the door that adjoined the bathroom and locked it, as well. Only then, convinced even Flynn wouldn't break down a door at his own resort, did she sneak to the bedroom window and move the curtains ever so slightly to see if he was still there.

He was, and the sight of him standing by the gate looking as if he'd been hit by a ton of bricks brought her great pleasure. She recognized that slow burn, that incredible sexual tension, and was glad she'd given it to him. At least she wasn't the only one feeling that burn.

Teddy, who she'd let out this morning before her

massage, came up behind his master and shoved his broad head beneath Flynn's palm, asking to be petted.

Flynn reacted absently, gently petting the black dog, before shaking his head and walking away.

FLYNN WENT to his den to recuperate.

He lay back in his leather chair behind his massive antique teakwood desk and wondered how all his plans could have come to this. She wasn't the same woman anymore. She seemed nothing at all like the girl he'd fallen in love with, like the woman he'd assumed he still loved.

And she turned him on like no other woman ever had.

Who would have thought that shy, virginal Alison Hennessy would have stripped off her clothes, totally and sensually enjoyed a massage, then dropped her robe as soon as she entered her seaside villa? Just the thought of her walking around naked gave him the hardest erection he'd had in months. And he had the feeling his fantasies didn't even come close to the reality.

What had happened to her during those eight years? How had she changed into this totally sensual, wild and daring woman? And why hadn't he been there to see those changes?

Flynn had to admit he'd been dead wrong. He'd thought that once he had Ally trapped on his island paradise, she would listen to him, believe in him again, realize that their parting and divorce had been a huge mistake. Now, however, she looked like a woman who was so strong she didn't even need a man in her life. The woman Ally was now could pick and choose among any man.

She'll probably have dinner with Hans tomorrow night. He stopped his train of thought, not liking where it was taking him.

Well, he'd acknowledged he'd played it all wrong, and he'd done so because he'd assumed he knew her. He wouldn't make that mistake again. Flynn realized he could take nothing for granted and that this woman would have to be seriously courted all over again.

Strangely enough, he found himself excited—and fascinated—by the challenge.

"SOME HOT BATH," Alison muttered as she quickly showered off all traces of massage oil. She was far too nervous for a nap or a bath. She had a lot to do before dinner with Flynn tonight.

When she'd packed for this vacation, she'd brought along clothing suitable for lying around a resort. There had been no thought of dressing for a man or even meeting a man, let alone Flynn. She'd mentally gone over her wardrobe the moment he'd asked her to dinner, and found it lacking.

So, after drying off and slicking her wet hair back beneath a baseball cap, she decided to see what kind of boutiques Paradise offered. The brochure she'd brought along told her there were several, and she'd bet money that Flynn, like most men, wouldn't know their inventory.

All Alison knew was that she had to find a killer dress and be ready by eight. A dress that reflected the woman she now was. And a woman she was getting to like more and more with each passing hour.

She grabbed her purse, let herself out of the villa and looked up and down the pathway that wove among all the tropical plants. Determined not to stop and study them and dream about how to arrange them in the most artistic way, she stealthily made her way to the main lobby and the stores just below it.

SHE CALLED HIM at six and changed their dinner time from eight to nine, just to knock Flynn off balance. And at precisely nine that evening, Alison let herself out her villa's door and started toward the restaurant. It wouldn't do to arrive too early, look too anxious. She wanted Flynn to have a chance to experience a moment of doubt. That oh-my-God-is-she-having-dinner-with-Hans moment.

Within ten minutes, she entered The Reef. Glancing around, she had to admit that Flynn had done a wonderful job.

The restaurant appeared to be underwater. Artful design made the small, intimate tables seem tucked away in various areas of an enormous coral reef. Of course it wasn't coral, just some material made to look like coral. Huge saltwater aquariums graced the walls, lit so the illusion of light behind water made it seem as if you were dining beneath the sea, in Neptune's Kingdom.

She wondered what Flynn would say when he saw her in this dress, because it was a little number that Alison Hennessy would have never worn before this trip.

Then every coherent thought flew out of her head as she saw Flynn coming toward her. As her heart sped up and her breathing quickened, Alison knew she would have to be extremely alert and on her toes to make it through this evening unscathed.

She wondered which one of them would be the winner.

4

HE LOOKED absolutely devastating.

Dressed in black pants and a billowy white shirt, he seemed like a fantasy come to life. His long hair was pulled back, bound with a slender leather strip. The gold earring gleamed in his ear, and her eyes widened at the sight of the simple gold cross on a chain around his neck.

She'd given it to him as a wedding gift, and Alison knew he had to realize the significance of his wearing it tonight.

Yet she refused to react, didn't want to give him that advantage. Instead she watched him carefully, determined to gauge the full impact of the dress she'd charged this afternoon in one of Paradise's exclusive little boutiques.

The saleslady had assured her that no one really dressed for dinner in the Keys, that casual outfits ruled on this group of tropical islands. So when Alison had found the slinky little black slip of a dress, the saleslady had assured her it was just the thing. She'd made the woman happy, buying both the dress and an armful of matching silk lingerie. She couldn't have imagined going to dinner in her standard white cotton underwear—not with a man like Flynn.

Alison had no illusions about this dinner. She knew that by accepting Flynn's invitation, there was a very good chance they were going to end up in bed. But that was another part of their relationship she wanted to test. She wanted to make love to Flynn one last time, say goodbye to everything they had ever been to each other and move on—with Teddy in tow.

If she was going to say goodbye to this man who had once been such a huge part of her life, she had to say goodbye to all the aspects of their relationship. And she was ready to do so tonight.

It seemed strange that she had only been at Paradise for two days and was already contemplating making love with her ex. It was almost as if she was doing the exact reverse of what she had done so long ago, making both of them wait for exactly the right moment, when she felt safe and secure and loved. When she'd said her wedding vows.

Well, she didn't feel safe and secure tonight. She felt wild and reckless and free, and she wanted to see if Flynn was as wild as she thought he was.

There were other people dining in the restaurant, and she realized that Flynn had kept this area of the resort open to the public. Strangely enough, she didn't feel any safer with him in a crowd.

He guided her to an intimate little table, far back in the restaurant, and pulled out her seat for her. She practically held her breath as he touched the small of her back, urging her along. As she sat in her chair her spine stiffened, the movement almost imperceptible.

Tonight, no matter what the decision, the choice would be hers.

"Would you like to start with a drink?" he asked as a waiter came to their table.

While the old Alison would have said no, the new Alison decided that a drink was just the thing.

"What do you recommend?"

"We do a mean Scorpion."

She smiled at him. If he wanted to try to get her a little loosened up, then she'd go along with the plan.

"I'll have one of those."

"Make it two," he said to the waiter.

The drinks arrived, and they both ordered their meals. Seafood, of course, The Reef's specialty, along with some spicy, Cuban-inspired appetizers. And within the hour, as Alison picked at her first course, she realized her ex-husband's potent sex appeal affected her just as strongly as it ever had.

"You look beautiful tonight," Flynn said as he sipped his drink.

She didn't question his sincerity. If he was trying to get her into bed, he was doing a damn good job of it. Though Flynn had never really had to try with her.

"So do you," she said, her voice low. "Good enough to eat."

To her surprise, a wash of color stained those high cheekbones, enough of a blush so she could see it in the low, romantic lighting.

"Would you excuse me for a moment," she said, wondering if she'd just lost her mind by blurting out her intimate thoughts. "I'm going to go to the ladies'."

She left her seat, walked away from the table and somehow found the restroom, where she promptly locked herself inside a stall, lowered the toilet lid and sat down, covering her face with her hands.

She wanted him so badly her hands were shaking.

But she didn't want to be so vulnerable with him. She didn't want him to see how he affected her. Because if he did, he would have the upper hand. Wouldn't he?

Something she had read a long time ago slipped into her mind.

The best defense is a great offense.

Perhaps it was time to state the truth. Surely there was strength in that? And the truth was, she enjoyed the thought of knocking Flynn off balance. Big time.

Alison sat for a while, trying to quell the inner shaking as she wondered what it was she was about to do. Because once she made this particular move, there would be no going back. Ever.

HE COULDN'T look at her without wanting her.

Flynn glanced in the direction of the ladies' room, already hungry for the sight of her. He wasn't hungry for food in the least; he could have skipped dinner entirely. But if he was going to seduce Ally, he was going to do it right. Spare no expense, and go all the way with every romantic gesture he could think of.

He'd arranged for his private suite to be filled with flowers. Pink roses, her favorite. And a bottle of very good champagne on ice. Now it was simply a question of whether she would put him out of his misery. In a way, he'd always known she was in charge. He'd never wanted to do anything she didn't want to do, and that had given her a rather singular power over him.

But he hadn't minded keeping passion in check—not for Ally.

He glanced up, saw her and took another swig of his Scorpion. The strong drink did nothing to quell his desire. Just looking at her, at that sexy body in that dress, at the candy-red gloss on her lips, at the sensual way she'd made up her eyes, caused Flynn to wonder if she had gone to all that effort just for him.

He hoped so.

She slid into her seat, flushed and breathless.

"Flynn," she whispered, glancing around as if she didn't want to be overheard, though this part of the restaurant was nearly empty.

"What?" The conspiratorial gleam in her eyes had him genuinely curious.

"Let's get out of here." She slid her chair closer to his, leaned toward him and whispered in his ear. "Let's do it. Now."

The blood seemed to be roaring in his ears.

"Do it as in—"

She leaned toward him again. Those red-glossed lips barely brushed his ear and whispered something so erotically explicit he felt his body leap to attention.

Flynn was not a man to question the presence of a miracle. He silently thanked the Gods, took Ally's hand and led her out of the restaurant.

The chef would understand.

HE TOOK HER HAND and led her across the grounds. The sun had already set, but the night air was sultry and perfumed with the scent of flowers.

"Where are we going?" she whispered, wondering if he would take her to his private lair. She knew Flynn had to have one. He was a man who needed his cave and retreated to it often.

He didn't say anything, merely hurried her along.

They reached one of the white buildings on the far side of the resort, and as Flynn took a golden key out of his shirt pocket and unlocked the iron gate that led to a secluded courtyard, Ally realized this had to be his private quarters. The thought thrilled her. She was finally going to see how Flynn lived, the home he'd created for himself.

She'd thought he was going to lead her directly to the bedroom, but the minute he locked the iron-grilled door behind them, he maneuvered her into a corner. He pressed her against a smooth, tiled wall, grasped her buttocks with his hands, hauled her up against him and lowered his mouth to hers.

It was everything she could have ever wished for in a kiss.

And it was different from all the other lovemaking they'd shared. Before these two days together, Flynn had always seemed to treat her with a reserved care, and she'd sensed he believed he couldn't push her too far. She'd wanted him to, but he'd treated her as a princess, a fragile woman who couldn't be allowed to know if there were any deeper, darker depths to the man she'd married.

He'd changed, and so had she. She wasn't afraid any longer, and responded to his kiss with a wildness of her own. This was no tentative parting of her lips. There was a barely restrained ferocity in this man as his tongue plunged inside her mouth, as he pushed closer to her, parting her legs, letting her skirt ride up her thighs as she straddled one of his.

She moaned against his mouth, then grasped those powerful shoulders, wanting everything he could give her and more.

He didn't disappoint her.

She heard the sound of ripping fabric and was shocked, then aroused by the sight of the torn strap of her dress. He pushed it down, exposing the fact that she hadn't worn a bra. Cupping her breast in his hand, he kneaded the sensitive flesh, then rolled the taut nipple between his thumb and forefinger.

He didn't give her a chance to respond before he lowered his dark head and took that nipple into his mouth, pulling on it strongly. Her head arched back as she exposed her neck and shoulder to him, more of her breast. His large hand came behind her back and seemed to pull her up, made her all the more helpless to his ministrations.

She was being taken. There was no other word for it. She barely had time to catch her breath before he was tearing the rest of her dress away, and she found herself naked to the waist in the moonlight. She fell back against the cool tile wall, breathing heavily, gazing up at him.

He looked like someone out of a dream, like the man who appeared in a woman's most erotic fantasy and ravished her. Like a pirate in days of old, wrecking and salvaging ships, raiding island villages. Finding her at home, alone, deciding to take what he thought was his.

They stared at each other for a moment, and she could see the rise and fall of his chest, the way he seemed to breathe as if he'd been running a race. His eyes glittered in the darkness, and as his gaze raked over her, she knew she'd never been so intensely the focus of any man. Flynn had never wanted her quite this way before.

Not knowing what was driving her, only knowing that it felt so right, she slipped her hands beneath the waist of what was left of her dress and let it fall to the tiled floor. She stood in the moonlight, her breath coming frantically, her heart beating so hard she could feel it in her throat.

She loved the way he was looking at her, loved the

way she had to look. Clad only in a black thong and black, thigh-high stockings, she leaned back against the wall and gazed at him, defiant and a little apprehensive at the same time. She'd never been alone with a purely male animal like this.

They weren't married. He wasn't her husband. She owed him absolutely nothing. Yet she had the feeling she was in for the best sex she'd ever had in her life.

He didn't disappoint her.

His hands reached out, slid over her shoulders, the feel of his fingers rough and callused. His grasp of her was strong and assured, and she closed her eyes in utter ecstasy as he cupped her breasts, squeezed them, measured their feel and weight. Then those hands, those magical hands, smoothed their way down her sides, until his fingers hooked the strap of her thong on either side of her hips and began to peel it down her body.

She saw no reason to pretend she wasn't ready for him. Desire had sprung between them so fast, so effortlessly, that she didn't need much in the way of preparation. With a flash of sudden insight, she realized Flynn had been thinking about this moment, fantasizing about it, as much as she had. He couldn't be this wild for her if he hadn't.

Emboldened by this knowledge, she reached for the fastening of his pants, swiftly unbuckled his belt, unzipped him, saw the strong, proud erection straining against his clothing. It thrilled her that she could do this to him. She closed her eyes and groaned as his knowing fingers slid up her thigh and parted her legs so he might find what he wanted. They had a past, and he knew what she liked, but this was different from any lovemaking she'd ever experienced with him.

She was ready for him, but beyond caring that he knew it. For one wild moment she realized they weren't going to make it to his bed, that they were going to make love—no, *have sex*—right here in this enclosed, private courtyard. The moon cast its light over the two of them; the ocean breezes caressed their bodies. Flynn peeled off his shirt, and the golden cross gleamed against the dark hair on his muscled chest.

She didn't really relish the thought of lying down on cool, hard tile, so she wasn't at all surprised when Flynn led her to a portion of the courtyard wall that had a small window cut out of it. It was just the right height that, if she bent from the waist, she could support herself.

She didn't speak, didn't want to break the strongly sensual mood as she heard him strip off the rest of his clothing. Then he pulled her into his arms, kissing her savagely as she felt that masculine hardness pressing into her, so close, so tantalizingly close....

He turned her, positioned her so she was bent at the waist, her elbows and arms resting on the window ledge. She laid her head on her arms, feeling totally exposed to his gaze in the night air. His hands grasped her hips and she shivered once, almost convulsively, knowing what was about to happen, what *had* to happen.

He positioned himself between her legs and forced hers farther apart. The image of the pirate, the rogue male, taking what he wanted without any qualms, rose dark and forbidden in her mind. Then his hands were between her legs, caressing, rubbing, gently opening her, finding the small heart of her, creating a wet-hot and wild sensation that caused her to move her hips and cry out, her arm muffling the sound.

"Say it," he whispered, his voice rough.

She was so far into ecstasy she almost didn't understand what it was he wanted.

"Say it," he said again, his voice dark and rough. Strained.

Then she remembered.

You stay the ten days, I don't come near you, don't touch you, unless you ask me to—

If he was going to claim her sexually, Flynn wanted to know, had to know, that it wasn't just the Scorpion talking, that this wasn't the result of too much sun, sea and liquor. He had to know she wanted him.

Two could play at this game....

Reaching between her legs, she found him, that hot, hard, straining part that told her how much he needed her, how much he needed what she could give him. She touched the hardened shaft, so sleek and strong, so powerful. She stroked him gently at first, then harder, quicker. She'd never done this before, never been this aggressive with him, but found that she liked it, liked doing this to him.

She knew she'd broken his control when he jerked away, grabbed her around the waist hard, then parted those feminine folds with his erection, sliding just the head inside.

She squirmed, frustrated, trying to move her body so she could take more of him.

"Say it." His voice was hoarse, and she knew the tremendous control he had to be exerting over his baser desires.

She squeezed him, caressed him with her inner muscles and smiled as he swore softly.

"You say it," she managed to gasp. "*You* say it,

Flynn." As far gone as she was, there was still a part of her that wanted him to beg.

A man in such a state has no pride, Alison found out, as Flynn said between gritted teeth, "Damn it, I want you!"

Then with one long, glorious thrust, he gave her what they both wanted.

It was as if all his control finally broke with those grimly muttered words. She would have fallen if she hadn't had the ledge to brace against and he hadn't gripped her tightly around the waist. Yet the sensations he evoked in her were glorious. She relished being treated as a fully sexual woman and not as a girl whose sensibilities might be offended.

He wrapped her hair around his fist, gently yet inexorably pulled her head back, bit her neck, kissed her lips, whispered sexually graphic words to her between kisses as he moved in and out of her willing body, the primal rhythm relentless, rushing desperately toward release.

His wildness gave her permission to unleash her own, and she moaned loudly, bit her lip, then screamed against her arm as her climax rushed over her and she came. His orgasm rushed to completion right on top of hers, then he leaned over her, panting, holding her up, both of them gasping for breath, feeling as if they'd run miles and miles and miles.

She started to slide down the wall, weightless and boneless, absolutely shattered after what they'd shared, and was utterly surprised when Flynn still had the strength to catch her in his arms and walk toward his home. The large, carved wooden door opened easily, and he carried her through the darkened house, up a long flight of stairs, then down a hall to a large room, where he kicked the door shut, then deposited her on a kingsize bed.

He didn't waste a minute, but was down on the bed beside her, his arms and legs entwined around hers, kissing her as if he were still starving, as if they hadn't just both pushed each other to explosive climaxes mere minutes ago.

"More?" she managed to ask between kisses, teasing him.

"More," he muttered, moving restlessly down her body. And then what he was doing to her felt so fantastically good that she forgot to think for the rest of the night....

THEY MADE LOVE all night long, and the passion they'd both bottled up for eight long years came exploding out. Alison wondered, as she lay in Flynn's arms toward the morning, if what they felt for each other could ever be denied again.

She noticed the bouquets of pink roses that filled his bedroom. The sight of them touched her deeply. She knew he'd remembered they were her favorite flower. The chilled bottle of champagne had been put to good use during the night, the bubbles tickling her nose and the cool liquid reviving them both between bouts of lovemaking.

As she lay in his muscled arms, she wondered if Flynn loved her or if it was only a bad case of lust. She knew she loved him, because her heart had opened up as her body had. For her, it was impossible to separate the two.

But Flynn? Now that he had her where he wanted her, she wasn't as sure of his feelings.

Oh, he cared for her. He ordered food and hand fed

her, insisting she eat and keep her strength up. When Teddy scratched at the door, demanding to be let in, he carefully led their pet down to the custom kennel he'd had built for him.

"It won't hurt him, just this one night."

She knew he meant for her to stay the following day and into the night, and Alison decided she didn't care. She was on day three of her vacation, and if she spent the rest of the time she had at Paradise in Flynn's bed, well, that was fine with her.

She didn't want to think about the future. Or the past.

She sensed Flynn wanted her to tell him what had happened to her during their years apart—and she knew she never would. Unless he was to commit to her again, and then she just might let him know that there would never be another man for her in this lifetime.

He took her outside to his private pool, with water slides and a grotto and a private bar. They cavorted in the sun like children, totally naked except for the waterproof sunscreen he insisted on rubbing over every inch of her body.

And he made her beg. He had her exactly where he wanted her, and she didn't mind. She saw the pleased, passionate expression in those deep green eyes as he forced the words out of her, as he made her ask him to do the most outrageous things to her. She loved him, so she didn't mind. But she didn't want him to know that—not yet.

And she wondered, deep in her heart, if this was the reason he'd sought out Suzanne back then, if a man as passionate as Flynn had needed a real woman in his bed, and not the insecure girl she'd been. For something had changed in their lovemaking, and she knew it had something to do with the fact that he sensed she hadn't given it all to him, the way she had when they were married.

Flynn was a man like any other, and he loved the challenge.

That thought depressed her, and she decided she wouldn't worry about it for now. She would concentrate on the days she had left with this extraordinary man, this man who had once been her life. She wanted him to be a part of her life, and that, Alison found, made all the difference. She'd found herself sexually with Flynn during this idyll, while he thought she had found herself at the hands of another man, or men, and was now sharing it all with him.

She knew this when she woke in the morning and found him watching her.

"What are you thinking?" she whispered.

"How beautiful you are," he said, moving swiftly, rising above her, lowering his mouth to hers, settling himself between her legs. Laughing at the appreciative sigh she gave as she felt the length of his powerful erection resting against her slightly parted thighs.

"Is that all?" she teased. In reality, she liked this new woman she had become during her vacation, and she had no one to thank but Flynn. If he hadn't driven her to distraction, she never would have found this part of herself.

"And how much I want…" He brushed his lips against her ear and whispered all the things he wanted to do to her. Even days ago, she would have blushed a bright red. Now, with a major shift in her sexual attitude, she simply reached for him with a wicked gleam in her eyes that told him she wanted the same thing, too.

But all the while, during the days they spent in bed together, she wondered what would happen when she finally left Paradise. And how she could ever think of building a life with a man she couldn't trust.

SHE WAS LANGUISHING in a tub of bubbles in Flynn's decadent bathroom when he walked in, a smile on his face.

"I need to go to Miami on business tomorrow, and I was wondering if you'd like to come with me. We'd spend the night there and return the following morning."

Alison was honest enough with herself to know that she didn't want to waste a single minute of the time she had left on Paradise apart from this man.

"I'd love to."

"Good." He eyed the mound of bubbles. "You look good enough to eat."

She'd deliberately gone for a frisky look, her hair tied up on top of her head, held with a leopard-spotted piece of fabric, her eyes lined with dark kohl pencil. She didn't want to give up her bad-girl persona just yet. She didn't want to bore him.

"You look like you have too many clothes on," she said, and smiled what she hoped was a saucy grin.

His eyes lit, their expression delighted as he reached for the bottom of his T-shirt and pulled it over his head with one swift motion. She leaned back in the tub, enjoying the sight of his muscled chest with its sprinkling of dark hair, his flat stomach and his clearly defined abdominal muscles.

His hands went to his cutoffs, and he unsnapped and unzipped. Then he stood before her naked.

"Do you come out or do I come in?" he asked, gazing at her.

She glanced at his swiftly stiffening arousal. "I think you should come on in and cool down."

He laughed at that, and climbed into the tub, where he soaped her back, belly and breasts until she begged him to stop.

"Tell me what you want," he whispered.

She loved Flynn when he was playful this way. Alison led him into the shower, where both of them rinsed the bubbles off their bodies, then took his hand and guided him to the plush rug in front of the marble tub.

"On your back," she said, giving his damp chest a push.

His eyes widened. "Am I to be your plaything?"

"Turnabout is fair play," she whispered, then laughed.

"I love it when you talk dirty." But he complied, lying on the rug, his long legs bent at the knees, his feet flat on the floor.

She crouched by his side, leaned over him, kissed him senseless. When he would have pulled her beneath him, she stayed his hand.

"Wait."

She'd never felt as free with him. Straddling his body, she positioned herself directly over his straining arousal, teased him, barely touching him with her most feminine parts as she continued to kiss him, caress his face.

"Don't tease," he warned her, his voice a low, gravelly rasp.

"I never tease." She gave him a swift kiss. "I always deliver." And with that, she slowly slid down his erection, caressing the length of it, enjoying the feel of it.

When he reached for her waist, trying to set a rhythm, she caught his hands in hers.

"Let me."

His eyes widened in appreciation, then closed tightly as sensation became too much to bear. She moved slowly, seductively, taking her hair down and letting its length caress his chest. Leaning over and whispering naughty words to him, making him hotter and hotter for his release, but holding it back, knowing that in the end it would be so much better for the wait.

His hips moved, thrusting up, seeking satisfaction, and she lowered her face to his, kissed his cheek, whispered for him to be still.

"Let me do all the work," she said, her voice low, deliberately seductive. A part of her wanted control because in so many ways in this current relationship of theirs, she felt totally out of control.

She took her time, sensually torturing him, until his control broke and he rolled her onto her back and drove into her, giving both her and himself quite a satisfying finish. Then he filled the tub again, threw in some more expensive bubble bath and poured them both glasses of champagne as she lit a few candles to create a romantic glow.

As she sat across from Flynn in the enormous tub and sipped her champagne, she wondered what was going on in his mind.

He wanted her to stay. It was strange, how he had the approval and love of his parents and siblings. He had the respect of business associates. He was more than content with the way his life had turned out. He was almost a personification of the American dream, with more money in his possession than he could spend in several lifetimes.

But he didn't have the one thing he wanted above all—Ally's love.

He knew she still didn't trust him. Well, perhaps that would all change once they made their trip into Miami.

In the meantime, what they had was certainly incredible. Much more than he'd bargained for. There was a part of him that didn't want to know about any other man she might have been involved with. Yet there was another part that wanted to know, had to know, with such a masculine urgency and necessity it shamed him.

He was ashamed he had such an old-fashioned attitude. Ally had obviously made the change from the innocent girl he'd once known who had been embarrassed to be seen naked in front of him to the sensual, exciting woman who graced his bedroom.

You can't have it both ways....

How well he knew that.

So he kept her in his private lair, kept her fed and warm and sexually satiated. Kept her so busy he was sure she wasn't even thinking about leaving. While she'd been sleeping, he'd retrieved their things from the courtyard, but he hadn't given her a moment to go and get other clothing. After all, she had no need for clothes during the time she spent with him.

He wondered how she would feel when she found out the real reason for their trip to Miami. It kept him awake the night before they left. It didn't feel right, deceiving Ally. But Flynn was a realist. He knew that if he told Ally the truth, she'd never make the trip with him.

And if there was one thing he still wanted, it was the

truth. He wanted the truth about their breakup and divorce to come out; he wanted it crystal clear to Ally exactly what it was her father had done to the two of them.

Because it was only then that they could ever consider a future together.

5

THE DRIVE TO MIAMI was spectacular, along a highway
that linked the various islands. It seemed to Alison that
they were flying over the ocean, laughing and talking
in Flynn's red convertible, the bright sun shining on
both of them. The names fascinated her—Big Pine, Pi-
geon, Indian Key, Plantation Key, Key Largo. They
crossed island after island, bridge after bridge. They
passed barbecue stands and bait shops and roadside
stands selling enormous cypress-stump coffee tables.
There was a lot of the usual highway tackiness, but she
didn't mind. Any trip was fun with Flynn at her side.

She liked the fact that the two of them were going to
take a little road trip and spend some time away from
Paradise. They'd always traveled well together, starting with their honeymoon in Mexico. During their
short marriage, they'd taken several weekend trips.

And inside his sports car was the perfect place to
talk.

She'd been watching a huge group of seagulls in the
sky, though she preferred the pelicans that hung out by
the docks to sample the day's catch. Without looking at
Flynn, she said, "Where are your parents sailing
now?"

"Venice."

"Venice!" It took her a moment to get her mind
around this concept. "How could they sail their boat
there?"

Flynn laughed. "No, I gave them roundtrip tickets and a ten-day trip there for their anniversary."

She thought about this, about how close Flynn's family had been even when they hadn't had a whole lot of money.

"Your dad must be proud of you," she said.

"He is."

It was on the tip of her tongue to ask him where they were going, not in the car but in their relationship. A part of her wanted to ask if she could remain in Paradise and spend her time landscaping the grounds, getting to know the tropical plants that grew so swiftly and bloomed so vividly in this hot, lush climate.

But she didn't. There was still the broken marriage between them. His infidelity. Flynn was fine for a fling, but she still wasn't sure she could depend on him the way a wife needed to depend on her husband. It was so strange, because Flynn had never let her down except for that one horrible moment in that shabby little motel. That one moment of weakness that had cost both of them their marriage.

"What are you thinking?" he asked softly, and she started out of her reverie. She'd forgotten how Flynn could sense her moods, almost read her mind. She'd loved it when she'd been in love with him. Things had seemed to flow so effortlessly between them. Now it unnerved her.

"About all the plants in Paradise," she admitted, not wanting him to know where her thoughts had really been. "There's a part of me that would love to get my hands on them."

"I should hire you," he said, his voice low and soft. And her heart sped up at the thought of staying longer, of being with Flynn. Something about this man, her ex-husband, would always be seductive to her, always call to her, like a light calling a ship home from its journey on the sea.

Or like a wrecker's light luring a ship to its doom along one of the reefs, letting it break up and then rushing in to divest it of everything inside.

Flynn had done that once before. He'd divested her of everything, taken everything away emotionally the instant she'd turned the knob and stepped inside the shadowy motel room. The instant she'd seen him in bed with Suzanne.

"A penny for your thoughts," Flynn said, and she had the uncanny sense that he knew exactly what she'd been thinking.

She couldn't possibly tell him, not when her thoughts were in such turmoil. For now, having a simple affair with Flynn would have to do, even if her heart sometimes tried to tell her something different.

"I was thinking," she said, turning to him with a bright smile, "that I'd love a piece of Key lime pie."

MIAMI, a city she'd never visited before, seemed like a riot of color, scent and sound. Flynn drove her around a little, then they had lunch at a small café overlooking the ocean.

"What time is your appointment?" she said, finishing the last bite of her Key lime pie.

"Three."

"Do you want to drop me off at a bookstore or something, so I can kill some time?"

He studied her for a long moment, and the strangest feeling washed over her, as if he were looking deep inside her.

"No. I want you to come with me."

That was certainly strange. She didn't quite know what to think of this new development.

"Flynn, I'm not going to run off and leave you in a strange city."

For a moment, she thought she saw the briefest glimpse of sadness in those green eyes. "I know."

She didn't believe he did. Reaching across the table, she placed her hand over his.

"I'll go with you if you want me to."

He was somewhere else, thinking about something else. She glanced at her dessert plate, picked up her fork, squished together some of the delicious crumbs of the shortbread crust.

"Thank you, Ally," he said suddenly.

A strange sort of fear washed over her, as if he were thanking her for the time they'd spent together in Paradise. As if he were saying goodbye. But she had another two days of this vacation, so surely that couldn't be it. The pie she'd eaten sat like a lump in her stomach, and she forced a smile.

"Flynn," she said, not knowing what else to say and deciding honesty might be the best policy. "You're scaring me."

"I'm sorry." He reached for his wallet, threw a few bills on the table and then took her hand. "Let's get out of here."

They walked along the beach for almost an hour, a beach much more crowded than the beaches at Paradise. When they returned to the sports car, Alison was surprised that they didn't head toward the gleaming highrises. Instead, Flynn headed toward a much poorer, neglected area of town.

When they pulled up in front of a seedy little stucco house, painted a faded pink and with a jumble of plastic lawn decorations out front among the crabgrass, she wondered what they were doing.

"Flynn, I don't get it. A business trip? With someone who would live like this?"

He must have seen the doubt in her eyes, because he leaned toward her, cupped her face in his hands and gave her a kiss that was so emotional, so passionate, so *sweet*, that she felt tears welling in her eyes as he broke it off.

"Flynn," she whispered, her voice breaking. "Tell me what's going on."

He wanted to. Oh, how he wanted to. He wanted to take that beautiful face in his hands, look into those clear blue eyes and say so many things.

I need you to trust me.

I need you to believe in me.

I need to put the past to rest.

Flynn needed all these things, and he was smart enough to know that what he was about to do would either help Ally make the decision to stay with him or drive her away forever. Because though she might want to go to bed with him, he knew she still didn't trust him.

Strange, how a man could face a howling sea and almost certain death and not be as emotionally afraid as he was at this exact moment.

He'd lost her once. He wasn't sure he could go through it again.

"Ally," he said quietly, not looking at her. Staring out the windshield at the row of decrepit houses, rusted trucks on cinderblocks in the weed-choked yards. "I need you to do something for me."

"Anything."

She'd made that decision with her heart, he was sure of that. And the smallest bit of hope began to fight its way through the fear.

"Will you come with me and meet someone?"

"Sure." She took his hand, squeezed it, and he was both humbled and amazed by the simple faith she still managed to have in him.

He didn't want to lose her, but he didn't really have her. You couldn't have what you'd never really possessed. Flynn was a realist and knew the way the world worked. He was going to go for broke in less than a minute, and even though his heart was pounding heavily, he knew it was the only choice for him.

"Let's go." He had to move. He had to get this over with. He got out and walked to Ally's side of the car, then opened her door and gave her his hand. She took it, sliding out of the front seat, and he watched her, studied every detail. The brightly colored sundress, green and peach, that billowed around her slender legs. The way she wore her caramel-colored hair down, sort of tousled around her face. The way he liked it. The slight gloss on those full lips, the high color staining her cheekbones.

It hit him, then, that she was as nervous as he was.

And suddenly, he wanted to know. He wanted to know if she could face the truth, and if, after she faced it, they had a chance at a life together.

They started up the walk, then some steps badly in need of repair. Flynn opened the sagging screen door, then rapped sharply on the peeling wooden door three times. He stepped away from Ally, let go of her hand. She was the only one who could decide if she wanted to go through with this. He wouldn't force her.

The woman who came to the door had brassy blond hair and a deeply lined face. Her hands shook slightly as she smoothed thick bangs from heavily lined eyes. Her face was puffy, her voice hoarse as she said, "Yeah, and what do *you* want?"

Flynn glanced at Ally. It was clear she had no idea

who this woman was. In truth, this woman could have passed him on the street and he wouldn't have recognized her.

"Suzanne Haines? It's Flynn. And Alison Hennessy."

Alison felt her stomach start to take a nosedive, and for one awful moment she almost turned and ran. The woman who stood in front of her, in a badly stained pink and orange housedress and dirty pink scuffs, bore absolutely no resemblance to the voluptuous, sparkling blonde who had married and divorced her father.

Who had slept with Flynn.

Who had destroyed her marriage. Oh, wait, Flynn had done that all by himself.

She stared at the woman, unbelieving. They couldn't possibly be the same person, this woman, this pathetic creature who stood in front of her, and the woman she'd been. The woman Alison had always believed she could never be for her husband. The woman who'd haunted her, made her feel totally inadequate.

Suzanne glanced at Flynn, then at her. A skinny, apricot-colored poodle, badly in need of a bath and grooming, came up to the screen and sniffed disparagingly, then offered a disinterested little whine. Suzanne scooped the small dog into her arms, sighed, then reached for the screen and opened it. She gestured for them to come inside.

"I've been thinking that one of these days the two of you might stop by."

IF THE OUTSIDE of the house looked decrepit, the inside was a disaster. They settled in the kitchen, and Suzanne didn't offer a pretense of preparing a cup of coffee or getting out a plate of cookies. From the empty bottles of alcohol filling the two garbage cans, Alison figured out how her life had been going.

"I take it this isn't a social call," Suzanne said, her voice hoarse. "Did Jim send you two down?"

"Jim's dead," Flynn said bluntly.

"Oh."

Alison noticed that the woman's hands shook as she picked up a red-and-white pack of cigarettes and a cheap lighter. She flicked it furiously, desperate to get a flame, and Alison didn't miss the quick sheen of tears that gleamed in the woman's faded blue eyes.

She took a deep drag on the cigarette, pulled an overflowing ashtray closer to her, then leaned forward and said, "So, what can I do for you?" The slight sarcasm that tinged her words seemed to put up a shield between them.

Flynn was silent as Alison watched him. Then he said, "I want you to tell Alison the truth about that night. The real truth."

Alison watched as Suzanne took another drag on her cigarette. She seemed almost defiant as she stared at Flynn. Then, as if in slow motion, the wrinkled face, hidden by layers of faded cosmetics, began to crumple. Her hands shook as she stubbed out her cigarette, spilling ashes across the table's speckled surface. Her shoulders shook, and she covered her face with both hands. Alison realized the woman had started to cry.

"I'm sorry."

The words came out as little more than a whimper, a strangled little noise that Alison felt as well as heard. Suzanne had carried around a lot of guilt and pain for a long, long time.

Alison couldn't look at Flynn as the import of the woman's words rocked her world.

I'm sorry.

Those two little words meant that it had all been a lie. And if it had all been a lie, that meant her father had lied to her about Flynn. He'd taken her away and urged her to divorce her husband, told her he was no good.

"You called me at home that day, didn't you?" she said, her voice little more than a whisper. "You told me where to look."

Suzanne nodded, unable to meet her gaze.

Alison glanced at Flynn, whose head was bent. He seemed to be studying a fast-food wrapper in the far corner of the kitchen floor.

She turned her attention to Suzanne.

"You didn't have sex with him." She pressed on, a sick feeling in her stomach. "He didn't come on to you."

She shook her head again, her hands still covering her face.

"Tell me."

The woman shook her head again.

"*Tell* me, damn it! You owe me that much!"

The nicotine-stained hands finally came away from that ravaged face. Suzanne took a crumpled handkerchief out of her housedress pocket and blew her nose loudly, mopped her face, smearing the heavy black mascara and liner.

"He came to the bar to hear his brother. He was playing in the band. Your daddy told me exactly what he wanted me to do. My sister needed help, there were some people after her, and...he offered me a lot of money."

Alison couldn't take her eyes off the woman.

"I wanted to help her."

"What happened next?" Alison seemed to hear her

own voice as if it hadn't come out of her mouth. It sounded flat and dead.

"I thought it would be easy, a man like him. You meet a lot of them in bars. But I couldn't get his attention. Oh, he knew what I was up to, but he told me he was a married man. He loved you so much."

Flynn quietly turned and left the kitchen.

A short silence, then Alison said, "Go on."

"Your daddy told me that if Flynn didn't rise to the bait, I was supposed to...supposed to take a pill and put it in his drink when he wasn't looking. I distracted him and opened up one of these capsules and stirred it into his drink while everyone was watching the band."

Alison thought she was going to be sick. She clenched her hands so tightly her nails almost broke the skin of her palms.

"Before he passed out, I asked him to walk me to my car. I...I told him I was afraid to go out in a dark parking lot by myself. He started to stumble as I unlocked the door, and I told him to sit a minute and clear his head."

"Then you took him to the motel room."

"Yes."

"Took off his clothes." Alison wanted to hurry the story along, get it over with.

"Yes."

"How did you lift him? You're not that big a woman."

"Your...your daddy helped me."

Alison closed her eyes as pain she didn't know it was possible to feel washed over her, numbing her. The whole story seemed so unreal. This woman and her kitchen, even her pathetic poodle, seemed like something out of a surreal nightmare.

"When you opened the door and he saw you, he was

frantic to get to you, but he could barely move. That pill was a lot more powerful than I thought.''

But just powerful enough, Alison realized, *to give my father time to get me out of town.* Looking back, she realized how skillfully he'd manipulated her, setting up the situation, encouraging her feelings of rejection and betrayal.

Orchestrating her entire divorce. Her *life*.

"He looked for you. He wrote you letters."

She'd never received them.

"He was out of his mind when he finally left town."

She hadn't known. The picture her father had painted of Flynn was that of a player, a man who had an insatiable sexual appetite. Who might have wanted the little wife at home but would always have a woman or two on the side.

She'd heard enough. But there was something she had to know.

"Was it worth it?" she whispered, her throat still aching. She felt as if she were vibrating with a very fine rage.

Finally, Suzanne looked her in the eye.

"No." She reached out a hand, and Alison shrank back.

"Can you forgive me?"

Alison stared at the woman, then stood up and started to cry. She grasped the edge of the grimy kitchen table and overturned it as Suzanne swiftly got out of her way.

FLYNN HEARD the crash and smiled grimly as he sat on the front steps. He'd felt like doing much worse when he'd found out that Jim Hennessy was behind the horrible night that had destroyed his marriage.

Well, now it was up to Ally.

She raced past him, tears streaming down her face, her skirt swirling around her legs. She leapt down the rickety stairs and began to run. Past the car, and right out of his life.

Flynn went after her.

He knew she had no idea where she was going, yet he wasn't prepared for the way she struggled when he finally grabbed her arm.

"Let me *go!*"

"Ally, look at me."

"No!"

He held her, easily overpowering her as she finally started to sob, clutching his shirtfront, her hands balled into fists. He cradled her against him, held her, soothed her with endearments, with the words he'd longed to say to her.

"Ally, don't. Don't do this to yourself. I love you, that's all that matters."

He felt tears fill his eyes as she continued to cry. He lowered his head so he could whisper in her ear.

"Darling, I can't stand to see you cry."

He carried her to the car, buckled her in, then started the engine and decided to take her back to Paradise.

SHE STARTED CRYING in the car, and Flynn pulled over at a coffee shop on the highway. Inside, he insisted she order food she protested she didn't want. Over soup and sandwiches, he finally got her to talk about it.

"When I saw you…" She stopped, looking at her conch chowder, and he could almost feel the tension in her throat. Flynn sat and listened.

"When I saw you in bed with her…I just ran." She pushed a shaking hand through her hair, then looked at him with red eyes. "I didn't even think about trying to talk with you, trying to understand…"

She was blaming herself, and he couldn't have that.

"It looked pretty damning," he said, keeping his voice soft. Low. She'd been through a lot today, and there would be more painful feelings as time went on. She would have to come to terms with some agonizing realizations that were probably going to be more painful than the original experiences.

"My father—" She covered her face with her hands. "Oh, God!" The words came out muffled, her shoulders started to shake, and Flynn slid out of his side of the booth and came to hers, put his arm around her shoulders.

"Your father has nothing to do with you. I don't blame you for what he did—"

"But I believed him, Flynn. I *believed* him!"

He didn't have to ask her what Jim Hennessy had said. All of it would have been pretty damning, he was sure. But what she couldn't forgive herself for was believing what her father had said—and not believing in him.

"I tried to find you," he said, taking her hand as she wiped her eyes with the other.

"My father told me that the best thing was to start over. He bought me a plane ticket, and I went to spend the next few months with my aunt in San Francisco."

No wonder he hadn't been able to track her down. Jim had made sure she'd vanished without a trace. He'd never heard of this aunt or he would have been on her doorstep, demanding to see Ally.

"What that woman said today—I can't believe my father would do such a thing, would decide to manipulate me that way." She pushed the bowl of chowder away, crossed her arms on the table and lowered her face into them. From the slight trembling of her shoulders, he knew she had to be exhausted.

"Come home with me," he said, stroking her hair. "Come home with me, Ally, and let me take care of you."

She turned her tearstained face to his. Those beautiful eyes filled with tears, that face he loved to watch started to crumple, and he took her into his arms and held her as she cried.

MUCH LATER THAT NIGHT, once Ally was tucked securely in his bed with Teddy resting protectively at the foot of it, Flynn watched her sleep.

He wondered how she would react if she knew he'd made a few wellplaced calls to a friend of his in Miami, a doctor who had once stayed at Paradise and who specialized in substance abuse. If things went according to plan, Suzanne would be checked into an excellent rehabilitation facility by the end of the week. Her poodle would get proper veterinary care and would have a home here at Paradise for as long as his mistress was healing herself.

He wouldn't tell Ally now, because it would take her a while to forgive Suzanne, just as it had him.

He studied Ally, watched her sleep and wondered.

Well, he'd taken a chance. He'd told her he still loved her, even though he wasn't sure any of it had registered because she'd been in such pain. Seeing how fragile and emotionally broken she looked, he wanted nothing more than to protect her from the world, to keep her safe from any further emotional harm.

But he also knew she had to face her demons on her own.

She stirred, then opened her eyes. They were still red from all the crying she'd done, but he could honestly say she'd never looked more beautiful to him. He leaned over her, balancing his weight on his elbow, then touched her cheek the way he had the first morning he'd seen her in Paradise.

"Hey, beautiful," he whispered.

"Oh, I am not," she whispered back.

He stroked her cheek, looked into her eyes.

"Flynn," she whispered.

"What?"

"I can't stand—the wasted time. All that time we could have been together." She hesitated. "We could have had a family by now."

He'd been thinking much the same thing.

"Ally," he said, treading carefully. "Why didn't you come to me? At least to argue with me, snap my head off, slap my face, something. You know?"

She looked away, and a few minutes passed before she glanced in his direction.

"I never thought I was good enough for you," she whispered.

"What? How could you have thought that!" The idea astounded him.

"Not…that way. I mean, I never thought I was good enough to…enough for you." She hesitated, then covered her face with her hands. "In bed."

Comprehension slowly dawned. Realization came to Flynn with a suddenness that almost knocked him back against the pile of pillows.

"You thought that I—"

"I thought you might have…needed a woman like Suzanne. Someone with a little more experience. Someone who could—"

"—satisfy me," he said, finishing her sentence. The final piece of the puzzle clicked into place.

"Do you remember Mexico," he asked, sliding closer, taking her into his arms. "That first night we spent together?"

"Yes."

"Do you remember how good it was between us?"

She hesitated.

"Don't think, Ally. Remember with your heart."

She smiled at him, a tentative smile that tore at his gut.

"It was magical." She hesitated. "Do you remember what I told you?"

He grinned at her. "That it was everything you'd thought it was going to be and more. And that it was worth the wait."

She nodded.

He slid his fingers into her hair, holding her head so she had to look at him.

"It was that good for me, too. It was always that good, Ally. I never needed, or wanted, anyone but you. Ever. *Ever*." He kissed her. "Do you believe me?"

She nodded. "Do that again," she whispered against his ear.

"What?" he whispered.

"Kiss me."

He did, then said against her ear, "Tell me what you want."

"Make love to me, Flynn." The yearning, the ache in her voice caught at his heart.

This time, it was different once again. This time, he knew he wasn't letting her go. She could landscape the entire resort or have twelve of his children, or none, or one, or whatever she wanted. But he wasn't going to let her out of his sight ever again.

He marveled at how wonderfully responsive she was in his arms as he kissed his way down her body, to her breasts, to her belly and below, creating that want, that need, that hunger that culminated in his rising above her and swiftly sheathing himself in her willing body. He rocked her, gently at first, then with more urgency, then suddenly it caught fire and both of them raced toward completion. At the last moment before his release claimed him, he held her tightly against him and said her name. Then afterward, as he relaxed against her, slid to her side, kept her in his embrace, he kissed her and kissed her until they lay curled against each other, totally spent.

And for that moment in time, Flynn was complete. He had Ally, and he would find a way to win her total love, no matter how long it took. Because he was nothing if not a fighter. He'd fought for his life on the open sea, he'd fought his way out of the agony of their destroyed marriage and built a business dynasty and he'd fight for her. Whatever it took, he was ready.

He opened his eyes and found Ally watching him.

"I have to ask you a question," she said, running a finger over the muscles in his shoulder.

"Anything."

"How did you get this?" She touched the scar on his chin.

He smiled at her. "An incredible storm at sea. The *Nemo* was just about to come apart, we were being buffeted by enormous waves, and I slammed my chin—"

"Flynn."

How well she could read him. He loved the laughter that was in her eyes and would do anything to keep it there.

"I was drunk one night in a bar. Thinking of you, of course. One of the bartenders, fortyish and a mother of five, offered to pierce my ear for me. After she closed the place down, she numbed my ear with an ice cube and used a needle."

"And?"

"I fainted." He smiled. "Hit my chin hard on the

way down. Don't tell anyone. You're the only person
who knows. Other than Nora, and I had to do away
with her."

She smiled, then reached up and touched his chin.

"Did you mean it?" she whispered.

He knew she wasn't talking about his scar. Or the
earring. She was talking about what he'd said to her
outside Suzanne's house.

"Yeah."

"Forever?"

"I always meant for it to be forever," he said, as his
heart picked up speed.

"Me, too."

Flynn pulled her closer, nestled her head against his
shoulder, stroked her hair.

"I built this whole damn place for you."

"I know."

"You do?"

"The way I figured it, how could you have stopped
loving me when I never stopped loving you?"

He finally had what he'd wanted for so long, something no amount of gold or buried treasure could even
come close to. He'd created Paradise, but it had been
nothing without Ally.

"If I'd found that ship," she whispered, "I would
have done the same thing. Built you a palace."

"You think so?"

"I know so." She kissed his chest. "I don't want to
leave, Flynn."

"I don't want you to." He took a deep breath. "I
want you to marry me."

"Okay."

"Okay? Is that all?"

"Yes."

"Yes, why?" Oh, he was feeling confident. And

cocky. He wanted to hear her say those words. He wanted her to say them for the rest of their lives.

She kissed his chest again, then wriggled her body until she was lying on top of him.

"*El Corazon de Oro*," she whispered, placing her palm over his heart. "The Heart of Gold." Her eyes filled with tears. "I'm so sorry, Flynn. I'll never doubt you again."

He felt tears sting his eyes, blinked them back. Funny, he hadn't even known how much he'd wanted to hear those words until she'd said them.

She kissed him, and he felt that wonderful surge of arousal again, swift and sure. Only this time it went deeper because he knew she loved him. He knew she had chosen to stay.

He caught her hand, held it against his chest until he was certain she could feel the way his heart began to race.

"You have my heart, Ally," he said. "You always have."

Then neither of them said a word for the longest time.

Heart of the West

*A brand-new Harlequin continuity series
begins in July 1999
with*

Husband for Hire
by
Susan Wiggs

*Beautician Twyla McCabe was Dear Abby
with a blow-dryer, listening to everyone else's
troubles. But now her well-meaning customers
have gone too far. No way was she attending
the Hell Creek High School Reunion with Rob
Carter, M.D. Who would believe a woman
who dyed hair for a living could be engaged
to such a hunk?*

Here's a preview!

and cry out, her arm muffling the sound.

CHAPTER ONE

"THIS ISN'T FOR the masquerade. This is for me."

"What's for you?"

"This."

Rob didn't move fast, but with a straightforward deliberation she found oddly thrilling. He gripped Twyla by the upper arms and pulled her to him, covering her mouth with his.

Dear God, a kiss. She couldn't remember the last time a man had kissed her. And what a kiss. It was everything a kiss should be—sweet, flavored with strawberries and wine and driven by an underlying passion that she felt surging up through him, creating an answering need in her. She rested her hands on his shoulders and let her mouth soften, open. He felt wonderful beneath her hands, his muscles firm, his skin warm, his mouth... She just wanted to drown in him, drown in the passion. If he was faking his ardor, he was damned good. When he stopped kissing her, she stepped back. Her disbelieving fingers went to her mouth, lightly touching her moist, swollen lips.

"That...wasn't in the notes," she objected weakly.

"I like to ad-lib every once in a while."

"I need to sit down." Walking backward, never taking her eyes off him, she groped behind her and found the Adirondack-style porch swing. *Get a grip,* she told herself. *It was only a kiss.*

"I think," he said mildly, "it's time you told me just why you were so reluctant to come back here for the reunion."

"And why I had to bring a fake fiancé as a shield?"

Very casually, he draped his arm along the back of the porch swing. "I'm all ears, Twyla. Why'd I have to practically hog-tie you to get you back here?"

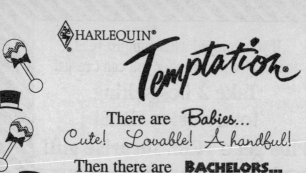

If you enjoyed what you just read,
then we've got an offer you can't resist!

Take 2 bestselling love stories FREE!

Plus get a FREE surprise gift!

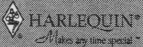

COMING NEXT MONTH

HARLEQUIN CELEBRATES

In August 1999, Harlequin
American Romance® delivers
a month of our best authors,
best miniseries and best
romances as we celebrate
Harlequin's 50th Anniversary!

Look for these
other terrific
American Romance®
titles at your favorite
retail stores:

**THE LAST STUBBORN
COWBOY** (#785)
by Judy Christenberry

RSVP...BABY (#786)
by Pamela Browning

**THE OVERNIGHT
GROOM** (#787)
by Elizabeth Sinclair

DEPUTY DADDY (#788)
by Charlotte Maclay

HARLEQUIN®
Makes any time special™